CW01080756

For my Grandma, thank you for always
didn't believe in myself. Lots of love, La~~~ ~~~

Laura had never had lots of friends; she always kept her guard up
and she made it difficult for anyone to connect with her. At forty-
three years old she was in a place she never thought she would be.
She had always been law abiding, well kind of.... she did break
some little laws that were harmful only to her and some bigger laws
that she had managed to walk away from but then she was clever
so her record had been squeaky clean, until now. She felt totally
betrayed by her ex best friend. As she sat in her little clapped-out
fiesta in the cul-de- sac she used to live in, the tears fell, and she
wondered why and more importantly **how** this had happened. Laura
was reeling. She was angry but she could not do anything about it.
Holding it all in made her blood boil. The police had warned her to
stay away and not contact Carla. Right now, she could envision
beating her to death with her bare hands. She hated the woman
who had once been her only long-term friend but that didn't upset
her as much as being made homeless and being cautioned by the
police did.

This had never happened to Laura before, despite the fact that Laura had done the same thing all her life she had never had to suffer the consequences and why should she? This was not her fault at all, it was all Carla's fault. They had been friends for twenty-three years but there had been a decade where their only contact had been through text and there had been times where they had very little contact, but in recent years they had been so close again, Carla always referred to her as her sister. Ha, some sister!

It had been ten years since Carla had seen Laura in person, but she knew that Laura needed her urgently so she had left her young children with a neighbour and had called another friend and asked for a lift because Laura lived around twenty minutes away by car. Carla was always loyal and even though this had been an inconvenience she had to go. Carla knew that right now she should be reading Ella and Cody their bedtime story, she knew she couldn't leave this, if she did then Laura might die. This was life or death and she knew she had to go. Carla was the only one who truly understood this sort of stuff, and she was the only friend Laura had told. She hoped she wasn't too late, she hoped that when Rebecca came for her that she would drive fast. Carla's heart was hammering in her chest, her mouth was dry and if she was honest, she felt sort of dizzy with the pressure of the situation. She had managed to convince Laura that she had no way of getting to her. She was a single parent who did not drive. "Oh God, please don't let her die, hurry Rebecca!" Carla was speaking out loud now in a desperate bid to not lose her head.

Laura sat there still on her phone, texting Carla, she had made her work hard to obtain her new address. She didn't think that Carla would actually come, she knew that Carla didn't drive. She sat there feeling sleepy, but her head was going at a hundred miles an hour. She was just about to give in and go to bed when she heard a knock on the door. It was Carla! Stumbling down the stairs of her one-bedroom flat, Laura didn't know what she would say to Carla, deep down she knew she had no intention of actually killing herself, she had taken more pills than she should but not enough to kill a woman of her size, let alone one with a tolerance to pain medications, but there were lots more in the Tupperware tub she stored them in. The truth was that Laura didn't want to die; she didn't know why she did these things, but this was what her brain had made her do. She couldn't help it. Deep down she had hoped that Carla would come, she wanted her in her life. Sure, she had work colleagues, she had acquaintances, but she needed someone loyal and she swore to herself that this time would be different. Carla wasn't like the others, she would never turn on Laura, she was empathic, she was soft and though Carla came across like she was cold, Laura knew that that was simply a front, a way of protecting herself. Laura knew that those barriers were down where she was concerned, and that Carla wouldn't betray her like **they** had.

Carla stood in the pouring rain, on the doorstep of a little flat. Her heart was beating so fast. She hadn't seen Laura in about ten years. However, she had many fond and fun memories from when they had worked together, with horses in a beautiful country park. She had known Laura could struggle mentally, it was something she understood, having bipolar disorder herself. A figure hovered at the door, taking off the locks one by one. Carla was so nervous, after all; she had said to Laura that she couldn't come to her but would need her address to tell someone the following morning to remove Laura's body. Carla hated lying, it made her feel sick inside, but to obtain her address she had to, so she told herself she had done the right thing. She was so scared that Laura would have internal damage to her kidneys and liver and knew that she should have called an ambulance, but she hadn't because she wanted to assess the situation for herself first.

Laura undid the locks on her door, Carla was much plumper than she used to be and was now carrying a walking stick, sure Laura knew she had a physical disability, she had known her since her teens but she wondered what had happened to make her friend this disabled, but now wasn't the time to ask, her head was in a spin because although she had sent the same "goodbye" text to a few people, some didn't even respond to it and she didn't think Carla could even get to her. It angered Laura deep down that no one else seemed to care if she lived or died. It made her feel unloved. Yet despite Carla being a single parent with no car, she had made it all these miles away. Laura really wanted to smile but she obviously had differing emotions and now wasn't the time.

Carla knew the stairs would be a challenge because of her disabilities, she still had them in her own house but was waiting for a bungalow and when at home she stayed upstairs often because of the toilet being upstairs. She couldn't let the pain show, she knew this wasn't about her and nor did she want it to be. Poor Laura, suffering to the point of not wanting to live and without any family to support her. Where were her family and why didn't they want her? she wondered. It was a question she was sure would be answered in the future. Carla felt she was the only friend that actually helped. She also thought that she was the only one that Laura would open up to. That responsibility weighed heavily on her shoulders, but as usual Carla only thought of Laura and her plight. The bearing this had on her was not of importance to Carla. This was about Laura; it was a delicate situation and Carla knew that she had to tread carefully.

Laura watched as her life- long friend struggled up the stairs, silently concentrating on every step, typical Carla though she never let anything stop her. It was a quality that Laura had loved about her, from the first day they met; she felt they were like kindred spirits, both with their own internal struggles but a sense of humour to pull them through it all. How amazing those country park days had been, sure Laura could only ride slow, lazy horses but at first Carla was the same, in fact the horse she bought was one of those steady, reliable cob types. Laura had been riding years though when she met Carla. But a riding accident had robbed Laura of her confidence. She didn't let it show. Back then their friendship had been different, they didn't confide in one another, in fact they basically ignored their problems and only ever let their guard down in later years, when Carla was old enough to get drunk. When they were drunk the barriers came down and this in a weird way had solidified their friendship. Sober though they both remained happy to the outside world and hid their misery with their twisted sense of humour. That was what had appealed to Laura, she believed Carla's head worked the same way as hers. She felt safe, she felt understood when Carla was around and deep down, she had known when she had sent that "goodbye" text that most of her work colleagues and horse-riding friends wouldn't come. The last time this happened no one came and Laura had been in a relationship then, her boyfriend had betrayed her, he called an ambulance and didn't even go with her he had even told them to "Just section the mad bitch!" Laura was drowsy but she remembered hearing him shout that as they had closed the doors of the ambulance. That was the beginning of the end of her and Kevin. But Carla had never let her down and the mere fact that she was here let Laura know that even with a ten-year gap of little contact she was dependable and a true friend, unlike her predecessors.

Carla tried to hide the physical pain that surged through her joints as she reached the last step, it always felt like an achievement to her these days, reaching the top of the stairs felt like reaching the top of a mountain, because to her the stairs certainly felt like a mountain. She made her way to the kitchen where Laura was filling the kettle and she gently took it from her and began filling it herself. Carla spoke as she did this, knowing that difficult conversations are far easier to have when you are not making eye contact. Carla was no expert in this and knew she had to wing it, but she herself had been in this mindset before and so she tried to be the person she had needed at those difficult times. The obvious question was what had caused this? But she decided to take a softer approach. "Laura what do you think would be needed to make your life better?" Carla was very aware that if Laura had taken as many pills as she had said then time was short but she needed Laura to open up to her, to trust her so that when she suggested going to the hospital and getting the medical care she needed, both physically and mentally, Laura would hopefully trust her and agree to go.

Laura couldn't believe Carla had come. It made her smile despite her deep sorrow. She had taken some of those pills and she cursed herself now that she hadn't taken them all. Carla had made the tea now and both settled on the sofa in Laura's cozy living room. Carla took Laura's hand and Laura's eyes brimmed full with the sadness which she had spent years hiding from the outside world. As she cleared her throat to speak, the tears spilled down her rosy cheeks and once those first few fell, the flood gates opened, Carla then embraced her and Laura broke in her arms. She couldn't put into words why she felt the way she did. She couldn't tell Carla everything no matter how much she wanted to, nor could Laura admit to herself why the things that happened to her always happened because she herself didn't really know why. Was there something wrong with her? Why did her father beat her when she didn't do anything? Why did he prefer her sister Amanda to her, even though Amanda wasn't his own flesh and blood? So, she just sat and sobbed. Laura worried now though that Carla would figure out that she hadn't taken a lethal number of pills, she made a grab for the Tupperware tub containing the rest of them, but as she grabbed them Carla quickly took them from her in one swift move, damn. Laura did feel desperate, her tears were real, they signified frustration and fear, anger, jealousy and utter rage and the only way she could show these emotions now were through these tears.

"Remember when you pulled me from the top of the building, you had lied saying you were going to hold my hand and jump with me?

Do you remember that Laura? Well now it's my turn, how many pills did you take? Shall I take all of these so we can die together and you don't have to go alone?" Carla knew that this way was not how she had intended to help her friend but she was out of ideas now as it became blatantly clear to her that if she didn't do something she would eventually lose her beloved surrogate sister. This was done to make her realise that overdosing and dying was not the answer. Carla now realised that she had to hope that Laura didn't call her bluff. Carla's heart was racing now. She had no way of knowing how many pills that Laura had taken but her instinct told her that it couldn't be many because Laura was still coherent and wasn't sleepy or slurring. Carla was a trained first aider but Laura likely didn't realise this. Carla awaited a response, her mouth went dry with the anticipation and for a few seconds she felt totally out of her depth, it dawned on her that at times when she was mentally ill her close friends must have felt this way too. Carla vowed to herself never to let things get this bad again, for her or for Laura.

"You can't kill yourself, you have your children, what do I have? I don't really have loads of friends, my family are all evil bastards so I don't speak to them, so called friends have betrayed me and left for one reason or another. Hell, I can't keep a man, even after ten years together Kevin lost it because of how I am mentally and looking back over my past relationships none have been good, they have all been cheats, liars and users. You have your kids; I don't even have any of those! There is nothing left for me, but I can't take you with me, it would be selfish. You can't do this! I will be ok. It will all be ok. Oh god I am going to be sick!"

Carla couldn't move fast so she got up in her own time, she could hear Laura gagging and spitting but not vomiting involuntarily as such. It didn't matter whether Laura had induced it, the tablets were coming back up and would no longer be in her system in a matter of minutes. Carla still wanted to make sure Laura had the psychological help that she so desperately needed, all she had to do now was convince Laura of that fact. Ha, that was easier said than done. One other trait they had in common was how unbelievably stubborn they could be, Carla didn't want to force Laura because she didn't want to put their friendship to the test. She made it to the kitchen area and rubbed Laura's back whilst reassuring her that she would always be there, and that Laura never had to face her demons alone. They were in this together and no diagnosis would deter her. They made their way back to the sofa and the conversation moved on to a much more lighthearted one.

"I can't believe you came Carla, how are you? Why are you using a walking stick and what happened?" Laura remembered how thin Carla had been, hell even children hadn't altered her figure, it was something that Laura was envious of once, although she never let on that she was to Carla. Carla was always on the go back then though, working 60 hours a week between two jobs, she had been on a showjumping yard before that and Laura had missed her at the country park trekking centre in that year. She was saddened to hear that Carla had had a rather nasty fall which had robbed her of her confidence, but she came back and began teaching the advanced showjumping lessons and her confidence returned and so just like that they were reunited. Laura had reached out to Carla before, on her last suicidal mission, Carla hadn't responded. It angered Laura at first until she discovered that Carla had in fact been being looked after by a family friend because her marriage had ended and this had led to her having a nervous breakdown. Laura had not even known how bad things were with Carla, Carla wasn't the type to bare her soul. They didn't speak for months because of this breakdown and when they had it had been via text. Laura always messaged jokes and the conversations over that decade had been lighthearted and fun. Carla hadn't leant on Laura back then; in fact, she hadn't relied on Laura's support since her teens. Laura did love Carla, like a sister really but their contact had not been face to face since the children had been born. Laura just didn't like children, she could just about cope when they were older but if she could get away with avoiding them then she did. It baffled her how women could go all gooey with babies and how they could be so naturally maternal. Laura wasn't like that, nor did she ever wish to be.

Carla tried to joke her way through telling Laura how a mysterious illness called Fibromyalgia had robbed her of her mobility and sanity, joking that the sanity had never been fully there to begin with. Carla was mindful that this wasn't about her it was about Laura. The conversation seemed to yo-yo between serious things and happier times that they had had in years gone by. Carla didn't mind this, it was Laura's way of being able to open up, sort of a little-by-little way of being serious about how she felt. Carla knew she had been diagnosed with depression, but she didn't feel that this was all that was at play here. Carla had been through the health care system where psychiatrists and the like were concerned, she knew that to get to the bottom of this was likely to be a long road fraught with frustration, pain and a feeling of loneliness and that Laura would need her support, not just now but in the future too. Carla never even questioned whether she was up to it mentally herself and just promised Laura that she would face this with her. She took out her mobile and called for an ambulance. She knew Laura was not likely to suffer any adverse effects from the pills she had taken but Carla wanted to be safe all the same. She also needed this to be recorded in the hope of getting Laura the help she needed, whether it be a diagnosis and medication or a talking therapy of sorts. Carla would of course always listen and she had a good understanding of where Laura's head was at but she didn't have the qualifications needed to help, an A level in child psychology wasn't going to aid her with a complex adult with unstable mental health.

Laura had agreed to the ambulance but now there was a knock at the door she wasn't sure. She knew that Carla was trying to help and that she was scared to leave her alone but it was now 11pm and Carla had to get back to her children. Rebecca was waiting outside in her car to take Carla home. Laura smiled at the fact that Carla had dropped everything without question to help her in her hour of need, which showed Laura she could be trusted, relied upon and was worthy of her friendship. She hadn't been completely honest with Carla because like the last time she did this, Laura had reached out to others earlier too. She didn't know if it was desperation that had driven her to do this or if she craved attention a little, it was a cry for help but Laura didn't fully understand why she did such things. Why did she lie to Carla tonight and say that she was the only one she could contact? Why did she make out she had taken more pills than she had? Was it to ensure that **somebody** came? Did it matter who, as long as she could offload all these things? She had explained to Carla that she wasn't speaking to her parents because after she split with Kevin they had the cheek to side with **him**! Kevin had made out that Laura was some sort of manipulative psychopath and they had believed him! Laura had tried to maintain a relationship with them in spite of this but hearing that they had met up with him to walk her beloved dogs had been all too much and so she vowed never to speak to them again, that had been a month ago. She had been on a rollercoaster since but she couldn't go into that fully, it was complex and messy and she didn't need to go into the details with Carla. The paramedics were here now and though Laura had known she would have to go with them she really didn't want to, her toxicology results wouldn't likely show anything up and she would be stuck in a waiting room all night long so after all the commotion she had caused, Laura decided she would not go with them and instead gave her details for the crisis team to call her. Laura had been here before, she knew the crisis team were useless and even when they thought you would take your own life they didn't care, they only took you to "The Orange Lodge" if you were likely to hurt others. Laura was certainly capable when the red mist descended upon her but now the mist had cleared, sure she was still angry and she knew that she would feel like she could explode with rage in the future. It was a certainty she had lived with for most of her life, the anger, the rage, the unpredictable mood swings. She was calm now; she had unburdened herself of all that she could for now.

Carla felt happier now, the paramedics had checked Laura's blood pressure and though they had asked her to go with them they were satisfied she was safe to be left. She wasn't illogical enough to be sectioned, that took the say of at least two doctors. Mindful now of the time, Carla knew she would have to leave at some point, she needed to get back to Ella and Cody, it was way passed their bedtime and her neighbour had them with her. Ella was seven, Cody was only five. They needed her there, tucking them in and reading them a story and as she walked down the stairs a pang of guilt hit her. Carla knew she had done the right thing by her friend, but her children had school in the morning and it was knocking on for midnight. She reminded herself that she was the only one that Laura could trust, the only one Laura could be totally open with, Laura had told her this much when she had been texting her earlier and with that thought in mind the guilt subsided. They both reached the bottom of the stairs and Carla turned to her long- time friend and hugged her, this seems natural to most people but to Laura and Carla it was something they only ever did when it was life or death, Carla didn't like physical contact with anyone but her children and Laura hadn't hugged anyone in years. Carla stepped out into the darkness and almost died with fright as she almost bumped into a couple who were around Laura's age that were stood on her doorstep. The paramedics were leaving now, and their headlights faded into the distance. The strangers greeted Laura as Carla left. This surprised Carla, she didn't even know who these people were and Laura hadn't offered introductions. She got into Rebecca's car and left.

Laura worried when she saw Leanne and Greg on her doorstep. She had messaged them of course and she had wanted them to come but their timing had made it seem like she had lied to Carla. Well, she had lied to Carla but only because she honestly thought no one was coming. Carla had arrived at around 8.45pm just twenty-five minutes after the first cry for help type of text. This had proved to Laura how much Carla cared, she was a single parent and within five minutes she had taken her children to a neighbour and sorted out transport. Whereas Leanne and Greg had waited almost four hours to get here despite being in the next village. There it was the anger was back and so the tears spilled. Deep down Laura knew the only tears she wept were those of rage or hatred, these were the only emotions Laura really had, though it wasn't something she could explain to other people and she had been desperate, that wasn't a lie but what she had craved desperately was attention; affection and someone to tell her how amazing she was. The people with her now had only come to clear their own consciences, she wasn't close to them at all, she knew Greg from work and Leanne had a horse at the same place that Laura had once kept Fizzle, the old, knackered cob that she had loaned for a year. If they had come here straight away, they wouldn't have bumped into Carla, because Laura would have ushered them away asking them to come back in an hour, once she knew Carla wasn't coming. This made her look bad and she knew it. Laura decided to get rid of Greg and Leanne, telling them that she had been checked over and was okay but needed to sleep off the effects of the pills. Once they left, she would call Carla and explain. Laura didn't know what she would say and decided to wait and see what Carla said about them showing up first.

Carla sat in the passenger seat of Rebecca's Porsche it had custom made heated seats, they felt more luxurious than her sofas at home, but then as a single mum her sofas were always preloved these days because she couldn't work now with all her physical difficulties. Carla didn't know what to think about the two strangers who had showed up on Laura's doorstep in the midnight hour, but she didn't feel it was really her business and nor was it the time to discuss it. Rebecca was eyeing her quizzically and although Carla didn't usually discuss her friends' issues with others she felt Rebecca deserved somewhat of an explanation, after all she had made her break the speed limit to get her here and she knew the gist of why it was so important to get there quickly. Carla also knew that Rebecca was questioning other things about this situation and decided it best to outline things. She wouldn't break Laura's confidence though, so she didn't divulge any of the personal details that Laura had shared. Rebecca had waited over three hours in her car while Carla had sorted Laura out. So, on some level Carla knew she owed Rebecca a short explanation of what had happened.

Rebecca didn't want to see Carla's mental health suffer, she didn't know Laura but she had known Carla for years and she knew how trusting she was, how vulnerable she could be underneath her cool exterior, Carla liked to act totally heartless but Rebecca knew it was about as far from the truth as could be and her loyalty to her made her overprotective. She had warned her on the way up here that she didn't think from the messages that it was genuine and it was at best a cry for help; of course, Carla had not been willing to chance that, that was what it was and had made Rebecca drive fast, even down the winding country roads! Rebecca didn't really mind, luckily the roads were quiet and it wasn't often she got to drive the Porsche that way and see how well it handled. She had sat with these thoughts for a few minutes before she spoke, deep down Rebecca knew that though what she was thinking was a logical viewpoint from the eyes of an outsider, it would still be hard for Carla to hear. Rebecca knew that getting Carla to take heed of her warning had about the same odds as Grimsby Town Football Club making it to the premier league, she still had to air her thoughts all the same.

"Carla I know you have known this woman a lot of years and have maybe been close in the past but there are a few things from what you have said about how she was and about the way things went in there that worry me. First off, you heard Laura gagging, but you weren't sure if she had made herself sick to stop her stomach from hurting, yet she told you she was going to be sick. When I know I am going to be sick, my mouth waters and out it comes, if she was going to be sick but then only gagged that makes me think she wanted to be sick but couldn't be, so she forced herself, but why? If she had said oh god, I feel ill and think I need to make myself sick to feel better, then I could understand it. Secondly, you got her an ambulance which she agreed to but then she refused to go with them. Why did she agree with you ringing one? Thirdly you said there were around a hundred pills in the tub you saw, if she wanted to die why didn't she take them all? I hate to bring this up but when you tried you took every single thing in your house didn't you? Finally, my fourth point, if you are the only person she trusts like she said in those messages and if she only told you as she had said, then who were those people on her doorstep? Did you call them?" Rebecca could almost see the cogs turning in Carla's mind and for a few minutes they sat in silence. She worried that by questioning the motives of Carla's lifelong friend she had upset Carla herself and she wondered whether to offer up valid explanations as a way of undoing what she had just said. As tempting as that was though, Rebecca knew that if indeed Laura was as much of a liar as what Rebecca believed she was then it was best she let what she had said lie, safe in the knowledge that if she was correct, no matter how long it took Carla to figure it out, these were words that may come back to her mind and help her to uncover the truth, Sure this could be in days, weeks or even years. So, she let the silence continue until Carla spoke.

"I don't know if she was sick or not but she looked rough and she said she took those pills, I don't know why she didn't take them all, I took all that I had when I did this, yes but maybe there was a doubt in her mind even if it was a small one, or maybe she forgot about those pills, I don't know. I don't know who those people are and I never spoke only to say sorry for almost bumping into them so again, I don't know who they were or why they were there, I didn't call them no. Look whether it was a genuine attempt, a half-hearted one or simply a cry for help I don't care, I am just glad she is alive and I have seen things from a new perspective. I am sorry you had to find me when I over dosed, Bex. I promise to never put you through it again. I will pay for the petrol and thank you for waiting all that time for me. I really appreciate it, you're such a good friend to me. I would hug you but you would be afraid if I bloody did and I would be worried if you hugged me back, we don't do showing our feelings do we and well, we are both a bit old to start that crap now! You are welcome to come in for a coffee but it's late and I know you have work and I will need to settle my poor kids into their beds, it's almost half past midnight. Thanks again Bex, Bye!"

Rebecca knew Carla's response would be something like this. It was typical of her, it wasn't so much that she had been blindsided, though she had been, at least a little in Rebecca's opinion, it was more to do with the fact that as usual Carla believed that Laura was as genuine as she was and had a heart as big as hers. Rebecca didn't believe for a second that Laura was genuine or a genuine friend. It was only three years prior to that Rebecca had got a text from Carla not saying goodbye but telling her what an amazing friend she was and how she needed to know that she is a good person, it was full of spelling errors and grammatical mistakes or lack of grammar at all, this wasn't like Carla who was always very proper with her wording, she always had been. Luckily, Rebecca had only lived a stone's throw away back then and had got there and knocked one of the children up and found her in time. Where was Laura then? She only lived four miles away, if they were so close that she only had Carla, then why did Carla not reach out to her and tell her what a good friend she was? Maybe she had but if that was true Laura hadn't been anywhere near, not then, nor during the aftermath. Deep down Rebecca knew her gut reaction was probably right but she knew how stubborn Carla was and she couldn't keep pushing this with her, it would get her no-where. Rebecca hoped she was wrong for Carla's sake and she vowed never to bring it up again. She would just sit on the fence with this and be there for Carla when she was needed. Never would she fly through the countryside again where Laura was concerned though, she was almost certain it was a cry for help at best and a manipulative way into Carla's small inner circle at worst. Rebecca chastised herself for being so cynical and put on some easy listening music for the rest of the drive home. She would always be there for Carla but where Laura was concerned, she reminded herself of a saying her mother always said to her, not my circus not my monkeys! Rebecca didn't know Laura and it would stay that way. She wasn't mad at all about having to go all the way out there, Carla wouldn't have slept and would have got herself into a state if she hadn't, Rebecca would do anything for Carla, she knew her friend had been through hell in recent years and she didn't need some mentally unstable and physically draining person in her life right now. This was Carla though, she had a hard as hell outer shell, yet was soft and kind- hearted on the inside. Rebecca smiled at the thought of how sensitive and loving her friend really was. She unlocked the passenger side door to let Carla out and decided to give her one final piece of advice; "Hey Carla, make sure you look after yourself, you know Laura is okay now and your children need you to not be stressed, they have to come first and so does your own mental well- being. Get some rest now."

"I will and Bex, you're a life saver, thankyou I knew I could rely on you!" Rebecca smiled and drove off. Carla was grateful that she had real friends like Bex. It was crazy how Bex had gone from being a pub landlady to a Veterinary Surgeon who specialized in saving the most hopeless of cases, but then at one time Carla had been a hopeless case and Bex had saved her. She wasn't jealous of her friend in anyway, Bex had a beautiful house on a private estate and her practice was only on the road adjacent to her country manor. Carla smiled at how money and success hadn't changed her friend, sure she drove a Porsche these days and not a clapped-out Convertible Astra, Carla smiled remembering how she had spilled a full cup of cola into the electrics of that car and all over Bex. They had gone to a drive thru on the way home from viewing a horse that Bex was thinking of buying, still miles away from home the car had spluttered to a stop and they were towed home! Bex laughed about it even though she wasn't exactly well off, she ended up not buying the horse and instead got another car, but never made Carla feel bad about it. The more Carla thought about all the good and bad times her and Bex had been through, the more she thought about the warning Bex had given her. Carla picked up her children and entered their home, she put on the kettle because despite the fact that Bex had told her to get some rest, Carla knew she wouldn't be able to sleep tonight.

Carla awoke with a start as her phone alarm rang out with a song by The Killers, she hadn't slept for long, she maybe got an hour and a half of sleep and her eyes were stinging and streaming. "Come on kiddywinks it's time to get up for school!" Carla always woke and could immediately function mentally, she had been a morning person for as long as she could remember, it irked a lot of her friends at times! Even on boozy weekends she had been on in her late teens Carla had woken early and wanted to go swimming or shopping to make the most of her day, hangovers didn't exist for her back then and she never wanted to waste a moment of the holiday. Carla's children, however, were not morning people despite only being young. This was something that was a blessing at times and a curse at others, on a Sunday it meant she often got an hour or two to herself before the pandemonium began, on a weekday it often meant physically lifting them from their beds, no mean feat for Carla these days! She decided that when she got the children to school, she would try and find some help for Laura and she would call her to ask how she was. If she needed her Carla would pay fifty pounds in taxi fares if need be, sure it was a lot of money for her as a single parent but she wanted Laura to know she had her back through this. It was a little triggering for Carla, but this was something she would only admit to herself. Carla wasn't at the point of desperation she had been when her husband had left four years ago but she remembered the utter devastation it had caused her very well. It had all gotten too much for her then and this was why she felt she understood Laura so well, they were kindred spirits, just as they had been years ago. Carla knew the system well and wanted to make sure that it didn't leave Laura without the help she needed as it had done her prior to her over dosing. Carla still felt a pang of shame when her mind drifted back to then. This was why she knew she had to help Laura, yes it did seem more like a cry for help rather than an actual attempt. This was why she had to step in now, before it became a real attempt and left her liver and kidneys in the same sorry mess Carla's were now in, or worse she was on a slab in a morgue. That thought sent shivers down Carla's spine and her eyes pricked with tears. She swallowed hard and pulled herself together in a typical mum style. Zipping up Cody's coat she braced herself for the cold November day and she opened the front door.

Carla's heart was hammering in her chest as the dial tone began, she didn't know why she was so nervous, but it wasn't often that she called Laura. They had previously only ever communicated via text message or social media so this was new for Carla, but she knew she had to call, you can't assess a person's mood by text message. Her hands shook, Carla may put on an incredibly good front, but she struggled with crippling anxiety and it wasn't easy for her to make phone calls. Of course, she did when it was necessary and this was definitely the case right now. Carla took a deep breath and silently reminded herself that it was Laura who mattered most now.

"Hi honey, how are you feeling?"

The concern was apparent in Carla's voice and Laura was glad she had rung. She had meant to call Carla last night but by the time Leanne and Greg had left, her head was spinning. Laura felt fine today and didn't really understand herself what she had hoped to achieve from last night's escapade. Was she suicidal? Had life finally begun to get her down? Was she just lonely now that Sarah was no longer her friend? Ugh Sarah! The anger was immediate at the thought of that bitch. Laura pushed her from her mind and cleared her throat.

"I feel fine, I meant to call you last night but I was so sleepy from all the meds I had taken, I am really sorry, apparently the crisis team at Norfolk General are going to call me but we both know that even if they do, they are useless don't we? That is *if* they even call me."

"I aren't the best at speaking over the phone or phrasing things well and I would rather just be honest and direct sweetie, do you want to die? Do you still feel hopeless?" Carla's mind was racing because she knew that it was unlikely that Laura's mindset had changed much with one visit and a good night's sleep. She needed to know how bad she was though; it was only that she wanted to support Laura the best she could.

"No, I don't think I do, I don't know how to feel really, I guess I am just numb and emotionless. I have cried all the tears I had, with you last night. Today I feel okay, just numb." Laura hoped she had come across well to Carla, she wasn't lying, she didn't know how to feel, how could she when she didn't even know what her reasoning was in summoning twenty or so people over last night? not that they all came of course!. She wasn't sure of anything anymore. She didn't know who she was, if she wanted to live or die, and why she did the things she did, was the biggest mystery of all to Laura. She couldn't lose Carla now, Carla had come, she had got all this way, she had left her family to be there, Laura loved her for this very much. Carla was amazing and this thought made a hint of happiness cross Laura's face.

"Do you need me to come over? I can do. If you don't want me to, then will you call or text me with what the crisis team say? Sorry if the questions are a bit much, your head must be pounding darling; I just don't want you facing this alone okay?" Carla never wanted anyone to go through these dark times without love and support, she knew how much it had meant to her. Her own head was pounding with the lack of sleep and she really could do with a nap but she doubted she would have time once she had cleaned the house, done the washing and ironing and prepared the tea. She would make time to see Laura though if she needed her.

Laura was pleased with Carla's response, it showed her how much she cared but she really couldn't deal with anyone today. Last night had been draining. Leanne had been so pissed off with her and told her she was selfish and that although they came to check on her, they didn't appreciate being told in the message that she had only messaged one person. Leanne had sent a message to a few friends of Laura's via social media to try and locate where she lived and discovered that she was lying about how many people she had reached out to at least. Laura had responded badly to being confronted but she did genuinely feel bad. At least she now knew why they had showed up together, but she wondered if deep down they had waited in the hope that she would die. There was no reason why they should want her dead, they hadn't fallen out with her but then Laura never thought rationally about such matters at the best of times; let alone when she was numb and tired like she had been by the time they arrived. Sure, they had softened when they had seen Laura's eyes fill with tears, Laura was angry with them but as always she never told them so and made out to them both that her tears were that of sorrow and frustration. In a way they were, she felt sorry for herself, mostly, she was frustrated but not with the world just the people she had as acquaintances who she had hoped would care enough to get there within minutes, to be proper friends with her like she wanted. As ever though she couldn't say this out loud. It was something that didn't even settle right within her, it made her seem an attention seeker and that wasn't what she was at all. Laura knew that to vocalize any of this might make people see her differently, that wasn't what she wanted either. Put simply Laura wanted to be loved, cherished, wanted, needed and relied upon. Leanne and Greg only came to clear their own consciences, to see her vulnerable and broken. No, Laura didn't give them that satisfaction. She had shed a few tears, dried her eyes and simply told them that she had sent them the text in error and she asked them to call her in the morning, when she was feeling more human.

"No Carla, please don't come over, all I have done is sleep, I am okay, honestly I am doing fine and I am so sorry about last night. I am going shopping today at some point and I am at an art class tonight so I will speak to you again later on. I will come and see you on Saturday, send me your address, I will explain everything properly then, when I have a clear head and will text you if and when the Crisis Team call me. Love you Carla, thank you so much!"

Carla was a little taken aback and not one to show emotion, she told her children at least twice a day that she loved them but her own parents hadn't really been that way. Even so it wasn't something she ever really said to anyone else. She did love Laura; she must do to have gone out there last night. Laura had been there for her once, when she was fifteen and so messed up she had climbed onto the top of a building, it was a confusing time that Carla would rather forget but she had found over the last twenty-four hours that a lot of things were coming back to her that she would rather not remember at all. It wasn't Laura's fault and she felt so bad for her right now, knowing that it was months before she herself had wanted to live again and it was years before she was thankful that she had survived. That time on the roof though, she had promised herself that if she ever got a chance to return the favour she would. She knew that this was a time that she could use her bad experiences to her advantage, they could help her to guide Laura to a happier life.

"Of course, honey, my address is 743 Freemans Avenue, I am still in the same old town, it's about a thirty-minute drive though so if you need me to come to you let me know, if not then I will see you Saturday! Oh, just one thing though, the kids will be here. I know you're not really a fan of children, but their father isn't involved so I have them all the time, even at weekends."

Carla awaited a response. When she was younger Laura had told her how she felt she wasn't normal, not only did she not feel any maternal feelings towards babies and children, she said they made her feel sick because toddlers get snotty, sticky and smelly and that she didn't just not want any of her own but that she had disliked any she had ever met. She had blamed her mother for this, she said her mother had told her in her early teens that she would amount to nothing but a pram-faced, teenage, single mum! Well, she sure had proved her wrong because that hadn't happened and Laura was now on the wrong side of thirty. Carla didn't want to force her to be around her children but given that she was a single mum and Laura worked a nine to five job, Monday to Friday, there was no other time. Carla really wanted to be there for Laura but if Laura wanted the close friendship that she seemed to be angling for she would have to get used to the children being around.

Laura disliked children it was true but maybe this would be different, sure she had been here before with Sarah's children, she had learned to tolerate them and even to feign some sort of love for them. It didn't come naturally, granted but she had managed to have a close friendship with Sarah, despite her also being a single mother of two. Truth be told Laura did not wish to feel the way she did about children but she couldn't really see the point in them. Why bring children into a world filled with cruelty and evil? Why had Carla? Carla had *known* evil. Laura wished she could have Carla to herself, the way it had been back when Laura was twenty and Carla was a mixed-up kid who craved a mother. It had just been them back then, but times had changed now and Laura knew she would need to adapt.

"Well, I don't expect you to lock them up in an outhouse or anything, it's completely fine, they are part of you so I am sure I will love them, I loved you as a kid didn't I? It's fine! See you Saturday, Love you, Bye!"

There it was again, she had said "Love you." Carla did not want to seem disingenuous but she also worried that she may come across this way whether she said that she loved Laura or not, simply because it made her feel awkward to say it to anyone. Ah she would have to say it back and hope it came across as natural, even though it certainly wouldn't feel it to her.

"Yeah, see you at the weekend honey, Love ya, bye!"

Phew she had done it, sure she had said love ya, in a blasé way, but hey it was the first time in her thirty-one years that she had said it to another adult who she was not in a romantic relationship with. It didn't come out unnaturally either because though Laura sounded fine, she couldn't possibly be as good mentally as she sounded, could she? Did anyone come back from the edge and feel okay? Maybe her feeling numb was a bad sign. Carla decided to make sure she texted each day until Saturday came around. Part of her was excited to get a chance to have a proper catch up with Laura but part of her was hoping that some of the unspoken questions she had had would be answered. Sure, Carla was very good at steering the conversation, but this was someone who was unbalanced mentally right now and she didn't want Laura to feel she was being dealt with, with kid gloves so to speak but she didn't want to be too direct either. Deciding to just see what happens and reminding herself that she was prone to over thinking things and that it never did her any good, Carla picked up her duster and got on with the housework.

She flicked the kettle on, now. It would soon be time to get the children, she had been quite productive for a Monday, she had done her housework and then helped her neighbour sort some of her debtors out. Carla had been a legal assistant and had picked up a few tips on how to speak to these sorts of people and how to mediate and reach agreements. She may not be able to work nowadays but she was always on hand to help out her friends and neighbours. She was pleased of the distraction if truth be told. All day her thoughts had wondered back to Laura though, not only because she was anxious and worried in case she wasn't doing okay and was struggling and not saying, but also because she couldn't ignore the fact that a few things didn't make sense. How had those people known that Laura needed help if she had only contacted Carla? Bex had brought up a few things last night that Carla had been thinking about all day. Why had Laura cut off her older sister and parents? She had mentioned that they had sided with her ex but why would they do that? Didn't he betray her when she was most vulnerable? She knew on some level that Laura's parents had been unkind, her mother with her choice of words and her father with his fists, in spite of that though Laura had maintained a civil relationship with them until she had split with Kevin. Another strange thing was why didn't she speak to Amanda now? Laura used to be close with her, she doted on her nieces, sure she didn't when they were small but after they reached the age of seven, she talked about them none stop. How lucky she was to be the aunt of two beautiful twins, how she had bought them a swing set when she was promoted from a lorry driver to office assistant for the haulage firm she had worked for. Sure, Carla had never met any of Laura's family because Laura was an adult and had been when they had first met but then they had been busy with horses and Carla's mother and father were always too busy to collect her from the country park. So, it didn't seem odd that she hadn't met Laura's family either. Maybe she was wrong to even question this stuff. This was her overactive mind at play and Carla didn't want it to come between her and Laura. Maybe she would get answers at some point but now wasn't the time to push for those and deep down, no matter how much the unanswered questions plagued Carla's mind, Laura was going through enough right now and Carla was sure that in time Laura might open up about everything and then it would likely all make sense.

The week had gone so slowly for Laura. She had called in sick on Monday because she felt dog rough. She had assumed that taking ten pills of a low-level prescription painkiller that she still had left from when she had damaged her knee wouldn't really do a lot, especially since she had put her fingers down her throat to bring them up. She still didn't know whether being emotionally void had driven her to want to die or whether it had prompted her to want to find a friend to make her feel loved, important and part of a family again. Her own family were not worthy of her, she knew that now. She just wanted it to be Saturday so she could spend time with Carla. Laura felt understood by Carla. She had once felt that about Sarah, her fist clenched seemingly on its own at the thought of her now. Carla wasn't Sarah, Carla really did care and Laura promised herself she wouldn't get wound up over trivial things with Carla. She had been too open with Sarah and then Sarah had used it to her advantage. Laura couldn't be best friends with someone who had remained in contact with her ex's and her parents, after Laura had told her why she wasn't speaking to them any longer. Why had Sarah ever wanted to know them? Why wasn't Sarah loyal to her! As angry as she was, part of Laura wanted to reunite with Sarah, but she didn't know if she could trust her. She had Carla now anyway. A car horn beeped and Laura was brought out of her daydream, realizing that the lights on the railway crossing had finally changed. What a hectic week it had been. Monday, she had enjoyed shopping and her art class. She had smiled practically all day. She didn't often feel happiness and there was still a feeling of numbness underneath but Laura had proof now that she had a friend who had never taken her for granted and who still after all these years, loved her enough to get to the middle of no-where in the middle of the night.

Carla loved her little monsters, but she sure loved it when they were tucked up in their beds. She had a lovely bubble bath, put on her best silk pajamas and her fluffy robe. She had been really preoccupied all week, but it was Friday now and Bex was on her way over for a Chinese take away and a glass of Sauvignon Blanc or two. This had been a ritual every few weeks. For Carla it meant she had some adult conversation, which was a rarity these days and for Bex it gave her a chance to get away from the serious nature of her work. They had become friends when Bex was a Publican, herself a struggling single parent back then. Carla had been eighteen then. Rebecca had often had to warn her to slow her drinking down. There was an age gap but only of nine years or so. Carla loved how Bex would bounce into her house, wearing her monkey onesie complete with tail! All the money that she had, but this was Bex, the same now as she always had been. It only made Carla respect her more.

Rebecca had been looking forward to her Friday night with Carla all day, her tummy rumbled at the thought of fried rice and fried chicken in sweet and sour sauce. It wasn't actual chicken, or at least Rebecca's wasn't, she was a vegetarian. It wasn't because she disagreed with eating animals but more that she hadn't ever liked the texture of actual meat. Sometimes they would share and Carla would have a meat free Chinese meal and other times they ordered separate main courses. Years ago, they would go halves or take it in turns to pay, now though Bex always insisted on paying. She knew that Carla struggled to make ends meet now that she was unable to work. Bex had been a cleaner for her before her prosthetics ideas had taken off and she had then been able to open her own veterinary practice. These days though she was far too busy and she had offered to cover the cost of a cleaner but Carla had insisted she was fine. Bex smiled, Carla could be laid with half her head off her shoulders and she would claim to be fine! Bex had performed life changing surgery on two dogs and a cat this week alone. She had also tried to remove a tumor from the lung of a ferret, not her usual surgery but no other veterinary surgeon would attempt it. The surgery itself had been a success, only for the poor thing to not come round from the anesthetic. It had made Rebecca's heart ache when she had to tell the old lady her treasured pet had not made it. She didn't charge for the surgery and made a mental note to send flowers in a few days' time. That was Bex, so soft when it came to animals. She was no one's fool when it came to people though. Even a slight untruth or an over exaggeration would make her distrust a person. She had once been as soft and as forgiving as Carla was but watching Carla's ex-husband manipulate and destroy her had been what made her alter slightly and when her own husband cheated on her with his teenage P.A. she put her barriers up completely. Bex had a few good long-term friends and she hadn't altered how she was with them. The thing was now, she had money, she was world renowned in her field and people knew who she was. This meant that everyone wanted to be her friend. She stuck with the ones who had been there for her when she was a struggling single parent, who had to put her studies on hold until she could afford the tuition and exam fees needed to qualify. Sure, she was close to forty now. Her daughter was grown up and had her own successful business and finally Bex had made it in life. Carla wasn't jealous or if she was, she hid it very well, she seemed to revel in every success Bex had, even minor ones. Rebecca knew she herself had a major flaw though, she couldn't for the life of her ever bear to bite her tongue. Sometimes she could be tactless. Sometimes with Carla she needed to be. Carla coped better with things if people were direct with her. The thing with Laura was still worrying Bex slightly, she didn't want to turn Carla against her she just wanted her to accept that she needed to be careful. The last thing Bex wanted was her friend getting hurt.

The Chinese food was arranged onto large platter style plates to fit all the different culinary delights on without them touching one another. Carla lived for these nights, the ones that reminded her she was more than just somebody's mother. The conversation was always easy and jovial between Carla and Bex and this often-alleviated Carla's anxiety. It was one of the very few times she knew she didn't have to worry about what she said or how she said it. Bex was straight talking herself and this meant that nothing could really offend her. They had expletive nicknames for one another and both women swore like sailors. Carla chatted openly about the weeks' events, nothing exciting really. Cody had drawn on the walls of his newly painted bedroom. Carla had only finished it a week prior. She had got her step sister to draw SpongeBob SquarePants and paint him and Patrick holding hands. Carla wasn't good at drawing but

Ashleigh was. He had found a marker pen and scribbled on the beautiful mural. Carla had felt like crying when she saw it but Ashleigh had said she would come and re do it all. That really was all that had happened. She waited to hear what Bex had done this week and was so delighted to hear of how she had made a cat mobile again after a bad collision with a car had left it with several fractures and how she had saved the leg of and elderly dog after it had taken a tumble down a concrete step and she had made a puppy with hip dysplasia able to run around for the first time in his life. Carla loved all the feel-good stories that Rebecca had to tell. They sometimes made her tear up but Carla seldom let them fall, mostly because Bex would take the mickey out of her for it.

Rebecca purposely didn't mention the ferret who didn't pull through, now and again if it was something which had happened that day she would tell the not so fun stories but as a rule Bex liked to see Carla laugh, she deserved to be happy and so any happy endings her cases had, she would share with Carla. Bex kept the conversation light for a while but she had to warn Carla what she felt about Laura. She wanted to be a little more tactful with it this time, so she chose her words carefully.

"So, have you heard from Laura since Sunday?"

Carla was taken aback by the fact that Rebecca had thought to ask about Laura, part of her felt that even though Bex hadn't met Laura she somehow disliked her. Although if it weren't for Bex then Carla would have been left at home panicking and in the dark about what was going on with Laura. Maybe it was just that after waiting three hours in the car, Bex was tired and a little snappy.

"She seems to be doing okay, she took Monday off work to sleep off the medication she had taken, she managed to do her food shopping and she went to her art class, which I am sure will have done her some good mentally. She said the Crisis Team didn't bother calling her back and no one has visited her at home either. I am surprised because although they can offer stupid advice over the phone at times, they do usually follow up on urgent referrals. I guess the National Health Service is stretched though and maybe someone forgot to call her or something. She is visiting us here tomorrow though so I shall find out more then, she did say she would explain in more detail about things then. I feel for her though, from what little she did say, her ex tried to have her sectioned and her parents are seeing more of him than they were her so she pulled the plug on them, mind you I don't think they were very nice to her anyway so maybe it's no big loss. Families are complex though aren't they, I know that more than most."

Rebecca, thought for a moment and pressed on. She wouldn't accuse Laura of lying it wouldn't be fair on Carla to insinuate that again, she had learnt her lesson with that one and this time she would just see what she could piece together herself. The trouble was she really didn't want to meet Laura, not because she was intimidated or jealous but because she couldn't be false with people, she would have to sit on the sidelines with this, for weeks, months, hell maybe even years?! But she would be better prepared to help Carla if she at least could work out if this woman was genuine and if not, she could at least work out what it was that Laura *did* want.

"Carla that was so good of you to disrupt your whole family like that, to help out a friend, particularly one you hadn't seen in such a while. You really are a good person, no matter how much you play the cold and heartless card. She is lucky to have you, I hope she realises that. I hope she gets whatever help she needs; did she mention any other friends she has as way of a support network? Or anyone you can call in an emergency if you can't get to her, after all I work, and aren't always available, what if it happens again and I am midway through a surgery or I am on call? I will always help you Carla, you know that I just worry that next time I might not be at home. I wouldn't want anything to happen to Laura after all, she is your friend, if she succeeded next time it would directly affect you. So tomorrow you need to try and get an action plan together of someone with transport who can get to her or you need to get her to agree to either dial 999 or allow you to call for help on her behalf."

Carla was touched that Rebecca had thought about this so intently.

Deep down Carla knew that Rebecca was probably looking out for her rather than Laura but all the same this was a sensible idea. I mean they hadn't been in close contact in a decade but Laura must have a next of kin, Carla knew that Laura had kept in contact with some old horse-riding buddies, she had mentioned them when the two of them had been reminiscing over old times. Carla immediately felt a bit of the weight lift from her mind knowing that having a plan of action would ensure that Laura was safe. There was another thing that bothered her, if there was any type of medical emergency, Laura lived alone and no one would know she was hurt unless she was in close contact with the neighbours, that was unlikely though or she would surely have texted one of them and not Carla. At least she knew how to broach the subject with Laura now in a non-confrontational way, just as Rebecca had, just then.

"Thanks for caring so much Bex, it has weighed heavily on me this week I aren't going to lie and some of the questions you had regarding Laura were probably valid. I think I will bring this up with Laura when she comes over tomorrow and hopefully it will make sense. I don't usually discuss one friend with another, which I know that you understand but I guess I had to tell you some of it anyway, to get me there. I know you only ever see animals all week and don't have any free time to talk to anyone else, aside from Danielle, so I guess I am okay to tell you this stuff." Carla laughed dryly, she knew Bex had her daughter, Danielle who she spoke to most days but aside from her, the only people Bex spoke to were other overworked vets and their only conversations were animal related ones. She knew Bex would take the joke in the lighthearted way it was intended anyway and she did.

The conversation went back and forth easily and Bex finished her fruit juice and went to put the kettle on, she knew Carla's routine now, two to three small glasses of wine with her meal and then a cup of tea before bed. Bex usually had 2 glasses of wine, watered down with lemonade then a fruit juice, followed by a cup of Earl Grey. Bex often brought her tea bags with her, this wasn't to be a snob, it was that Carla didn't actually like fancy tea, she was happy with her local supermarket's own brand. Coffee was different, Carla loved the Brazilian coffee beans that Bex always had imported especially. Bex ground the beans herself in a morning, it was worth getting up early for. On the odd occasion that Carla came to the Manor, Bex would encourage her to drink as much coffee as she wanted and would always grind her some beans to take home.

Carla sat with her mug of tea warming her hands. Her house had finally started to warm up, though it felt like it had taken all day. She had been wanting to say something to Rebecca all night but she wasn't as good at talking about her own feelings as she was at talking about animals, or film stars. Carla had promised herself she would say something though.

"Bex, I know we don't really do deep and meaningful shit on a Friday night but I really wanted to tell you something I have been thinking about since all this stuff with Laura, I am really glad you saved my life that night you know? Because of you I have been able to make memories with my kids, visit nice places and appreciate nature. I really am thankful now, you're alright you know, for a posh old tart anyway!"

Bex smirked at the last remark, it was almost comical that neither of them could give one another a compliment without following it with an insult but they were so similar like that.

"That's okay, I kinda had to save you, no one else will share Chinese food with me and chat utter crap on a Friday night, so it was really a selfish deed to be honest, plus you're the only person who is simple enough to find my jokes funny! I am glad you're still alive, corpses might look more with it than you do most days, but they don't make the best conversationalists, if truth be told!"

They both giggled and finished their tea. Bex watched Carla up the stairs before she left, it gave her peace of mind because Carla usually went to lay on her bed to watch t.v. once her children were in their beds. It was for safety because she had suffered several fractures from falls down that steep staircase. Bex would lock the door behind her and post the keys through Carla's letterbox.

Carla slept that night all the way through until morning, she was only woken by her Springer Spaniel Daisy, licking her cheek. It was 9 a.m. and the sun peeked thru the gap in her curtains. For a minute Carla forgot it was early November, her electric blanket made it easy to forget that it was. She pulled herself up using the handle attached to her bed frame and swung her legs over the side of her bed. Brrr it was bitterly cold, but she knew she couldn't lay there forever. Daisy wasn't the spring chicken she used to be and wouldn't wait much longer to go out before she started barking which would wake up the children and destroy the half hours peace and quiet Carla usually enjoyed with her morning coffee. She grabbed at Daisy's collar which had a sort of handle on it. It meant Daisy could help Carla down the stairs. As her difficulties had progressed, Carla had rescued the cute Spaniel from a puppy farm where she was used as a "breeder". Carla trained Daisy to do all the tasks she couldn't do and to help her with things like stairs. They slowly made it down the stairs, Carla signaled to Daisy to pick up the house keys from the doormat, she did so and dutifully passed them to her master, they went to the kitchen. After she had opened up the French doors for Daisy, Carla flicked the kettle on and took out some of the ground coffee Bex had given her. She needed to wake up fast today. Carla needed to get her carpet cleaned this morning and do a little housework before Laura got there. She was nervous and she said a silent prayer hoping that Ella wouldn't be the sarcastic delight she had become in recent times. Ella wasn't seven mentally, she was more like a petulant teenager who gave her opinion without it being asked for. Cody though was the polar opposite, he rarely spoke to people he knew, let alone strangers, he was young for his years and he was a mamma's boy. Carla reminded herself that if Laura didn't like her children, she really had no place in their lives. The children came first, and they always would do.

Laura woke up excited, she was going to visit Carla today, she was in a great place mentally now, all she had really wanted was a friend. Not like Leanne and Greg, they didn't really know her, not the way that Carla did, they didn't care as much and Laura deserved someone who made her a priority in their lives, Carla had already proved that she would do that. Laura wasn't sure how she would cope with the children being there, she hoped that they could occupy themselves so that she and Carla could have a proper catch up. Laura was good at putting an act on when it came to children, after all, most of the clients at the local country park's riding centre had been children and she had worked there voluntarily for years. Eileen had never offered to pay Laura, but then all Laura really did was answer the phone and sit in the office. It wasn't hard work; the instructors and their helpers worked the hardest. Eileen did reward Laura though with free rides. Laura always rode the same, fat lazy, cob there. He was just too lazy to be used in the trekking centre but Eileen was too attached to sell him. Laura had been secretly very jealous of some of the instructors there, the helpers were all children or young adults, Laura had been able to influence them very easily; often getting them to do unkind things to the instructors or even to other helpers that she didn't like. Laura loved those days; she was never mean to Carla though and she never let Carla find out about any of the "pranks" she had set up. Laura would never let anyone hurt Carla, but she never let Carla know when she had taken care of something and it always looked like these children just decided not to work there anymore. Laura loved Carla, she always had, and she probably always would. This was why today was so important, it was imperative that she try to connect on some level with Carla's children, she needed this to go well, she wanted Carla in her life.

Ella and Cody had laid in today, as always. Ella would be going to her dressage lesson at teatime, but the lady whose pony she was riding would collect her and drop her off afterwards. Carla usually went to watch but of course today she might not be able to make it. The carpets were looking better now they had had a few stains removed, all her cleaning was done and the only smell in the air was the faint whiff of bleach. Carla loved her immaculate home, she would in a way be sad to leave it. She took pride in her house, even though the extent to which she cleaned, often left her almost bed ridden. It was 10.30am when Carla took the carrot cake out of the oven and placed it on the cooling rack, as she did so, there was a banging as though a herd of elephants were rampaging down her stairs. Cody, she knew it was him because anytime food was cooking, he made an appearance, it even seemed to rouse him from his slumber. Cody was half asleep but still managed to string a sentence together, probably because it also involved food! "Mummy please can I have cake for breakfast?" His beautiful blue eyes were pleading with her, but Carla still needed to add the vanilla frosting on the top and it needed to cool. "Sorry baby, you can't have cake for breakfast, besides its not cooled or been iced yet and it's for when mummy's friend gets here."

Cody frowned but accepted that he wouldn't get any cake until later. Carla smiled to herself, he was such a cute kid, even when he pouted. She hoped the colourful cereal would be a consolation to him and judging by his face now, it was. "Where is your lazy sister, is she still in bed?" Cody nodded while taking another mouthful of cereal. Carla really needed her to get up so she could get breakfast over with in one sitting and then clear it all up before Laura came. Carla felt nervous butterflies in the pit of her stomach and then she felt an excited sickness too. She was nervous because she was always anxious that her house wouldn't be clean enough, Carla always felt this way; particularly when the visitor was someone who didn't have children. Other tired, stressed-out mothers didn't expect a palace and accepted the mass of children's toys but when childless people were coming it tended to put Carla on edge and send her into a mad cleaning frenzy! It was worth it though. Laura had never visited Carla at this house, or in any of her previous residences. They really didn't need to back then because they spent every weekend together and also met up in pubs for nights out. This meant that this would be a first and as usual this made poor Carla panicked and slightly shaky. She knew that she needed to get bathed and sorted because Laura would be with them in an hour and she wasn't likely to be late. One thing Carla remembered about Laura was her punctual nature. She still had to set out Cody's clothes and bath him. Luckily, Ella could bath and dress herself and no longer allowed Carla to help. Typical of a girl of that age but it saddened Carla because it signified that Ella was growing up.

Laura had a little bother finding the house, it was on a lovely little cul de sac but it was in an estate where Laura wouldn't wish to live, she didn't have the means to have a big house to herself so she rented a one bedroomed flat in a tiny little place with no shops, no parks and most importantly no children; the whole village was made up of about twenty houses and Laura had checked prior to moving there whether there were many children, she knew she didn't want to live next door to any. The landlord owned half of those twenty properties and assured her the residents were all hardworking couples with no children or retired couples who had no children residing with them. She had grown up in an estate worse than this but had lived in villages all of her adult life. Laura had moved around a lot in that time, apart from the decade she had lived with Kevin. They had lived in a lovely large bungalow in a quaint little village where everyone knew everyone. Although she liked villages, Laura hadn't ever mixed with any of her neighbours, Kevin had, but then he had lived there all his life, he had inherited the property the year before they had met. Laura didn't really want to mix with people, she didn't want people knowing her business, at first she may have been open to it but, since she had likely been the talk of the village she didn't want to hear what people said about her. She and Kevin had to drink in a pub in the next village, even so, Laura was still sure that people there were talking about her. She had moved out of there to the little flat in another village on the outskirts of Norfolk. She never strayed too far from her roots, she had been born in Holt, and hadn't ever moved too far from there, apart from when she went off with a married man. They had had to escape his scorned wife and indeed half of Nick's own family. It wasn't something Laura relished thinking about, it always made her think of how it had ended and how she narrowly escaped prison. That was in the past though, Laura didn't see the point in having regrets, it wouldn't change anything.

Carla was now looking human again and the children were bathed and dressed and playing in the dining room. Carla's house wasn't big by any stretch, but at times she was grateful of the separate dining room. It meant that the children could play while Carla got some much-needed adult time and, as it was the adjoining room, she would hear if there was to be any squabbling. Carla really hoped today would go well and she hoped that Laura could answer some of the many questions that Carla's last visit had left her with, but she reminded herself with that thought that she shouldn't pry.

Laura cringed at the swing set, slide, trampoline and playhouse in the large front garden. She told herself that she had to resist reacting this way when she met the little brats. Laura really wanted Carla in her life and she would have to accept her children or feign that she liked them at the very least, well she was here now. Laura scalded herself for her thoughts and reminded herself that these were Carla's children, if they were anything like her then Laura would likely grow to love them anyway.

Carla had put the kettle on, just as she heard the doorbell. She went to the door, checking her appearance in the hall mirror on route. It has to be said she was nervous, although Carla dearly loved her babies, she knew that Laura didn't have a maternal bone in her body, True as it was that when Carla had met her, Laura was twenty years old, and Carla had been a child of around twelve, but with her traumatic life Carla remembered now that she had not acted like a pre-teen and was in fact a grown up in the body of a child. Her nerves returned with this thought but it was too late now, Laura was here. Carla took a deep breath and opened the door.

Daisy wagged her tail with such exuberance that her whole back end wagged. She had come a long way from the dog who was terrified by strangers. Carla thought this was a good omen and she knew that although not keen on children, Laura loved dogs more than any other animal and it showed. She looked upon Daisy with kind eyes and seeing this made Carla relax.

"Sorry Laura, this hairy beast is Daisy, she's friendly and clever, you will love her I promise. The children are playing in the dining room but will no doubt come through to be nosey, come on in!"

Laura loved the little spaniel who had made up the welcoming committee, and it was clear that Carla was pleased to see her. Laura could smell home baking; the aroma took her back to the days when her grandmother would spoil her with sweet treats. Laura couldn't help but smile, as the memory of her crossed her mind, her grandmother had really doted on her only grandchild. Her older sister wasn't sired by Laura's father and her only grandmother had been on his side. Carla's house was huge to say it was a housing association home. It was clearly one filled with love and for that, Laura was rather proud of Carla. She could hear a racket coming off of the lounge and it made her feel uneasy, but Laura didn't show it. She took a fizzy caffeinated drink from her handbag and opened it, Carla had offered her a hot drink but all Laura ever drank was fizzy drinks, this was why she was a size twenty-eight but it never bothered Laura, after all she wouldn't be the one carrying her coffin!

The door of the dining room swung open and in came Ella, Cody followed closely behind, but realising that he didn't know the lady sat across from his mother he had gingerly clambered onto Carla's lap and was hiding his face in the nape of her neck. Ella spied the visitor with a questioning look and Carla knew she would have to control this introduction before Ella's clever mouth took over. Carla actually loved her wise and sarcastic daughter and she didn't want to curb her personality too much but she knew from past experiences that where "new" people were concerned, she couldn't let Ella's smart mouth run the show because her daughter didn't have a filter or really care for the feelings of strangers. Carla knew that if Laura stuck around, she would inevitably be on the end of Ella's quick wit one day, but for now and with Laura not being mentally stable, Carla would have to take control of the conversation. "This is Ella, Ella this is my friend Laura, are you going to say hello?"

"Hello Laura, my mother says you are an old friend, are you even older than my mum then?" Carla was about to apologize when Laura started laughing.

The laugh had not been false, Laura immediately felt at ease, Ella definitely had her mother's dry sense of humour and Laura knew she wouldn't struggle to be around a child who was just like Carla had been. "Well compared to you I guess I am a bit of a fossil yes; I can't be older than your mother, I think she must be at least *fifty*!"

Ella laughed at this and said, "She is thirty something, she only looks fifty because Cody gives her wrinkles, I don't, obviously because I am perfect!"

Carla wanted to tell Ella not to be so bloody cheeky but part of her was relieved that Ella had made Laura laugh and had won her over. "Right, I think I need to ice this cake, or if you two promise not to eat any, maybe you can quickly help me? Sorry Laura, I didn't get chance before you arrived but I know you smoke so if you need to you can go through the French doors into the back garden, it's a bit more adult than the front garden and there is an adult sized garden swing or some seating, I promise we won't take long doing this!"

Laura wondered if Carla should be carrying Cody with her back the way it was but she didn't feel it was her place to say and she knew Carla wouldn't thank her for telling her not to do something. Carla had always been fiercely independent. Laura sat in the garden, though she was proud of the mother Carla had become, part of her was a little jealous too. Not of the children of course, in fact Laura couldn't think of anything worse than that but she did feel strangely envious of how those little people took up Carla's time but also of the love that seemed to come so easily to Carla. It was almost like her past experiences hadn't altered her. Laura knew that her own experiences had and that this was likely why she had no maternal feelings at all. Laura blamed everything that went wrong in her life on her upbringing and her useless, abusive parents. She had to snap herself out of this train of thought before it made her rage grow. She had decided that because she now couldn't easily trust people, she had to make this work with Carla and if the rage against her parents didn't subside then she would have to do something about it before it ruined what could be her last chance at happiness and her chance of being part of a family. Pulling herself together again, Laura put her cigarette end into the bin and walked back in through the patio doors.

The rest of the afternoon went really well and even Cody had finally started to come out of his shell, the children went back to playing in the dining room after their dinner and Carla didn't really get any answers but it was like the questions didn't matter anymore, Carla did mention the action plan idea and though Laura appeared skeptical about it she did seem to take onboard what Carla had said. They had reminisced about the old days, Carla could no longer ride horses and though Laura had done until recently, she had no plans to return to the saddle right now so all the two of them had now were memories.

Laura did take what Carla had said about a next of kin on board but she had no close friends, she felt she may have burnt bridges with Sarah and at this moment in time she still hated Sarah and resented her. Laura knew that she would likely do whatever it took to get Sarah back, just as she had done years before but right now she was okay, she had Carla. She didn't dislike Ella; in fact, she really liked her cheeky and confident personality and was impressed that at only seven years old she was having dressage lessons with an up-and-coming rider who was well known in and around Norfolk. Laura didn't feel the same optimism with Cody though, he sure was a mummy's boy and he seemed demanding and clingy. She did inwardly congratulate herself at faking that she was interested in him and that she liked him as much as she had Ella. Laura was relieved when Ella took him back into the dining room to play so that the adults could talk because faking being nice was hard work. Maybe she would grow to love him but right now she couldn't stand the little brat. He had his mother's attention every single day and she was worried at one point that Carla would barely get a proper catch up with her. Laura promised to visit in a few weeks and told Carla she would message her later. Walking away now, Laura smiled to herself, apart from the brats this had been just like old times and she felt like she and Carla had never been apart.

As Carla tidied away the tea pots, she thought about what a lovely visit it was with Laura. She was wrong to think that Laura wouldn't like her children and the whole visit had been full of lighthearted chatter and laughter, in fact it had been a world away from the last time they had spoken. Laura must be so mentally strong to put aside those suicidal thoughts and act like everything was fine. Carla's heart felt so full of love for the friend who had once been her savior, the happy memories flooded her mind and made Carla feel so happy, like the void that her friend had left in that decade where they hadn't seen one another had once again been filled. Their friendship had rekindled so easily and there was not an ounce of awkwardness between them. As she tucked Cody into his little car bed, Carla felt so lucky to have him and Ella in her life, for the first time ever Carla looked back on her troubled beginning and knew she had truly turned her luck around. After tucking Ella in, she let Daisy outside. They climbed into bed and then Carla fell asleep with a smile on her face.

The next few weeks and months flew by and Laura visited Carla frequently. Laura was also making friends in the office and finally felt that she was feigning a somewhat normal life. She didn't miss the moaning voice of her mother or the harsh treatment that she suffered at her father's fists. She did miss Amanda and she was secretly haunted by the way she had spoken to her sister the last time they had met. Laura had regrets and she did have some sadness in her, though it was herself she felt the most sorrow for. All Laura had wanted was a loving family, it was clear now she would never find that with her own family and she began to look on Carla as her family, Laura had even managed a bond with Cody, sure she was never maternal with them but she fulfilled the role of a loving surrogate sister and aunt, in a way, her inner child needed these interactions more than she realised.

Carla had a lovely circle of friends and had reconnected with her old horsey friends from the last yard she had her old pony on. She took Cody for riding lessons at the riding school there on the odd occasion. Laura came to watch and seemed to revel in Cody's milestones and made friends with the instructors. It was a lovely family run yard and Laura was welcomed with open arms.

Carla and Laura had been back in contact for around six months when Carla's world was turned upside down by a phone call. It turned out that someone had called the NSPCC and reported her for supposed child abuse and neglect. The very thought of this made Carla's stomach turn and she knew that she would have to be investigated. The next eight months forced Carla to the edge of sanity. It left her with a nervous twitch and a lack of belief in the local authority. During this time Rebecca and Laura were absolute angels and somehow, they got her through it. Ella and Cody now closed down and refused to speak to teachers and social workers because they saw that it made their mother so stressed out and they hated seeing her cry like this. They had told the truth about how their mother treat them but it was either twisted or landed on deaf ears and so they stopped communicating with anyone outside of their family. Carla had laid awake night after night, wondering who hated her enough to make up such horrific allegations Never had Carla raised her voice let alone her hand to her children. They were her everything! The worst thing was the false allegations would be kept on file and anytime her children hurt themselves, Carla would be under suspicion because it would flag up on the doctors' computer; if they went into school with any injury it would flag up there too. Carla's heart broke every time Cody scraped his knees or fell from his bike. She panicked now when she saw Ella climbing and had banned them both from playing outside. Whoever had reported her had known the children's ages and address and had really painted a terrible picture which had not an ounce of truth in it and it meant that Carla was as untrusting of new people as her children now were too.

Laura knew that the hoax callers' allegations had almost destroyed Carla and she tried to alleviate some of the pressure, she even took Ella and Cody out for the day so that Carla could have a break and try to get her head together, for the sake of her children. Laura had actually enjoyed those days and she realised the children loved her and held her in high regard.

Carla dared not admit to herself how close she had come to giving in. When things were at their worst and social workers were twisting things and using her disability against her, Carla almost took her life, but as she was contemplating it Ella had appeared.

"Mum, I know I am just a kid, but I don't know why all of this has happened. I know you're a bit poorly, but we can help you and Daisy dog does. You are the best mum you can be, and we love you for it and those nasty liars who make you cry will go away soon!"

Not long after this the calls and allegations suddenly stopped and though this brought Carla relief, nothing could undo the irreparable damage it had caused them all, both individually and as a family.

Carla suddenly realised she needed to fight this and that now the social workers were no longer on her back it was time to pick herself up. She knew it would have a lasting effect on her and her children. Though the truth was, that she had only told Laura and Rebecca, too ashamed to let anyone else in. Carla felt like her reputation as a mother was in tatters and was sure that the teachers who had ultimately sided with the local authority, now judged her on a daily basis. As always though, in public Carla didn't falter. Deep down she knew she was a good mother, she wasn't perfect, but then who was? Children don't come with an instruction manual and really, she knew she was just winging it, as was every other parent she knew!

Laura was impressed that Carla had bounced back from a truly horrific year. It had been a hell of a rollercoaster for them all. Laura had almost got used to her phone ringing now rather than a text. Carla would always try to mask how broken she felt but most of the time she would inevitably end up in tears. At times Laura had become frustrated with it all and had ignored her phone. After all Carla had other friends, whereas Laura only had her. It almost made Laura jealous and though Carla had tried to integrate Laura into her inner circle, all it really did was spark off the possessive nature that Laura was trying desperately to control, or at least contain this time.

Carla had just about recovered from the crisis of the past few months; she had been accused of everything from drug use to alcoholism and child abuse and neglect. Now though she knew she deserved a focus. The first thing she did was book a caravan holiday on the Norfolk broads for her and the children. She worried about leaving Daisy because she needed her help with a lot of manual things; so, she paid extra for a pet friendly caravan, this way Daisy could come with them. Carla was looking forward to the holiday, just the three of them, four, if you included Daisy.

Laura was outwardly supportive of the idea of Carla taking the children away for a short holiday, deep down though she felt like an outsider for the first time in over a year and a half. It was a stark reminder that no matter what Carla had said about her being like family, there would always be times that she would feel forgotten; times where the children would come first. Laura thought that if she suggested a better holiday further away then Carla would need her to drive. Part of Laura hated her own idea, spending a long weekend in a tin can with two bratty little shits who were waited on hand and foot didn't sound fun in the slightest. But the idea of having little contact and not being included made Laura panic that she was losing Carla.

Carla felt very guilty when she and Laura met up, Laura suggested going much further afield than half an hour down the road. Carla liked going on the train though and Cody loved them, it was all part of their holiday experience. It wasn't that she didn't want Laura around, I mean she was constantly at the house, she spent Christmas with them and stayed right through to the New Year. Carla was very aware that she was all that Laura had and so she did usually involve her in everything but now, after the traumatic time the three of them had endured as a family, they needed time to recover, time to breathe. Carla was unsure now how she could break it to Laura without hurting her feelings. Laura had been betrayed by Sarah a few years back and the last thing Carla wanted was for her to feel she had done the same (all be it in a small and unintentional way) but she knew she had to put her children first and so Carla told Laura that they didn't want to travel far because Cody wouldn't want to sit still for long and they liked the train and wanted to just have a long weekend with just the three of them and Daisy, but that she would keep her phone on at all times in case Laura had a wobble with her mental health; she tended to every few months or so. Carla almost relented and invited Laura, but she knew that this time she needed to be selfish and think only of her children and indeed, herself.

Carla had a surprise for the children upon their return, she felt excited about this and hadn't told anyone that wasn't involved in organising it.

Laura finished work for the week and sat alone in her flat. She was angry at Carla for leaving her behind, she felt alone, her mind began to wonder, she could use this time to expand her circle. Laura devised a plan to get Sarah back in her life. She thought about her sister too for a fleeting second, before she stopped herself from getting too lost in that thought. It was too late to get her parents back and she would not want to, she was full of resentment and hatred for them, but she missed Amanda terribly. It wasn't that Amanda had taken sides or anything it was just that she was in the wrong place at the wrong time when Laura's anger had spilled over. Laura had not meant the things she had said or done that day but there was little point in regretting it now, sometimes things are just impossible to undo. Laura missed Carla and often wondered what they would be doing without her. The caravan was an 8 berth because Carla needed space to get around. Hell, Laura would have happily slept with Daisy! In fact, the dog was beautiful; and dogs were something that Laura could love instantly and indeed missed being around. An angry sorrow sat within her as she counted down the days until their return. Carla would be so happy when she realised that Laura had booked the week of her return off work. They could go shopping and bond even more, just as sisters are meant to. Carla was her sister now, she wouldn't let anyone treat her the way Amanda had allowed her father to, and Laura was full of resentment for her biological half -sister, once more.

Carla had really enjoyed the time away at the caravan, it had been so much fun and the children had loved the night times where they got to stay up and watch the entertainment. She was exhausted of course because it had been four days of none stop fun, which was far more than her now failing body could cope with. Carla didn't care how many days of rest it took to get her right. All the pain she felt now was worth the carefree smiles she had seen for the past few days. As they travelled on the train home, she smiled lovingly at her children who were suddenly silent and had fallen asleep with their heads together.

Laura stared at her phone in the hope it would ring. She knew Carla would be on her way home now. Although Laura knew Carla would much rather pay a taxi than ask her to pick them up, so she was unlikely to call until they got home. Laura imagined the three of them walking in the house with Daisy and the children going and putting on a film or cartoons to watch. Then Carla would put on the kettle and call Laura. Laura didn't care about their holiday and wasn't really waiting to hear details of their "family time," all she really wanted was to hear her sister's voice on the line. Carla was everything to Laura, so she often told people of her sister. She had never referred to Amanda as this. Amanda was only her half-sister anyway and she didn't understand Laura the way that Carla did. Carla was her family and Laura was sure that her phone would begin ringing any moment now.

Carla had not meant to fall asleep on the sofa and reminded herself she had to get the children into bed if they stood any chance of making it to school tomorrow. She let Daisy in the garden and climbed the stairs hand in hand with a very sleepy Ella and Cody. She would turn everything off and lock up now, that way, she could get an early night. She had to sort out the transport for something she had organised to be delivered for her little angels on Friday. It was something big and arranging everything would take a few phone calls and a few favours from Carla's friends.

Laura got ready for whatever she and Carla were going to do but she couldn't help but be seething mad as she did so. She broke the mirror with her fist and winced at the pain. She had never been good with pain but she always claimed to have a high pain threshold like Carla. It gave them another thing in "common" even though it wasn't really true. Sometimes Laura didn't know why she lied about little things because she and Carla had an unbreakable bond. Laura reminded herself of this and it seemed to bring a sense of calm to her. She would forgive her "sister" for not calling her yesterday because Laura had to, she often had to forgive Carla for things that she had never received an apology for. It wasn't Carla's fault, she had a lot on her mind, she had the little brats to think about. Laura was calmer now but she often got angry just by thinking of Carla's children and yet part of her liked them too. Laura was there first, she had known Carla longer than anyone else that she knew of and she had been everything to Carla, now she knew she wouldn't come first ever again and the thought made her blood boil.

Carla had woken up late and though she was tempted to keep the children at home, she couldn't because it may ruin the surprise. She spent most of the morning making phone calls and reconnecting with old friends. The butterflies in her tummy remained as she nervously thought about what she had actually gone ahead and done but along with nerves she also felt happy, like a missing piece of her had returned. Before she knew it, it was time to pick up the children from school. So, she called Daisy and off they went.

Carla stopped by the park so that Cody and Daisy could tire one another out. There would be no amazing home-made tea tonight. Carla had lost an entire day before she had realised it so tonight it would be hot dogs and chips. She always felt like a bit of a failure when she had to resort to this; but the truth was her body was still overcome by pain and she just couldn't stand up for long enough to cook something proper. Ella and Cody were thrilled that they weren't being forced to eat vegetables and it meant they could eat as soon as they returned. They could go to bed earlier than usual, in the hope of catching up on sleep.

Laura's disappointment in Carla was spilling down her cheeks now, why didn't anyone love her, the way that she loved them? She had thought about picking up the phone and calling Carla, but she knew it was no use, she would be reading to the brats right now. Did those spoilt little bastards even appreciate all the time that their mother gave them? She doubted it. They demanded it and Carla gave in to their demands, especially Cody. Cody was so attached to his mother that it almost surprised Laura that he hadn't tried to climb back up her fanny. The disappointment had quickly been replaced once again by anger and Laura did nothing to stop it this time. She would call Carla. It was the only way she could stop the hatred spilling out and ruining everything.

Carla sat with a book in one hand and a cup of cocoa in the other. She relied upon Ella to know when to turn the pages. This was a learning strategy to make Ella read along. Carla knew Ella was ahead of her peers, both academically and in maturity, Helping Carla may have contributed to this but Carla had always felt that Ella was an old soul. She seemed to understand feelings above a child's comprehension, and she was very close to her mother. Carla was so proud of the caring, compassionate child that her daughter had become and as she read, Cody's eyes began to close. He was a truly beautiful child. He had white, blonde hair long black eyelashes and the most beautifully piercing blue eyes. It was at bedtime that Carla most appreciated her children, she went to sleep every night, feeling blessed to have been given them. Now regretting reading to the children downstairs on the sofa and knowing that she couldn't carry Cody tonight, Carla took both his hands and led him slowly to bed. Ella followed sleepily behind them.

Carla had just let Daisy back in when her phone vibrated on the worktop. It wasn't late but it sure felt it to her. Carla glanced at the phone; it was Laura. Damn she had meant to text Laura today but the day had just flown by. Carla never ignored a call from Laura. She was tempted to tonight but then she chastised herself for even considering it. Tired as she was, Carla answered with as much energy in her voice as she could muster.

Laura hadn't known what she was going to say when Carla picked up the phone, she couldn't well tell her how angry she was that she had wasted a day off, sat by the phone waiting for Carla to make plans. Laura knew that she couldn't blame Carla for not making plans because she had likely presumed that Laura was at work; but then again, she hadn't called yesterday when they were both home either. Laura was sobbing her heart out now and her whole body shook as she did so. She knew she would have to either try to explain herself or make up another reason to save Carla from feeling guilty for letting her down. This was why she lied, to protect others, she lied to ensure that the friendship remained strong. Laura hated lying and if anyone lied to her then they were dead as far as she was concerned but sometimes Laura couldn't explain that her tears were caused by anger, so sometimes she had no choice but to lie.

Carla's heart hammered in her chest as she listened to Laura's distress. She should have remembered to call; she should have realised that something was wrong and she hadn't. Carla stayed calm in her voice and kept her tone even and soothing. She often had to do this when her children were upset, but then their problems were solved far easier than Laura's could be. The crisis team were useless so she knew she couldn't call them. Right now though, she felt that Laura was unraveling and fast! She had offered for her to come and stay. Carla would even give up her bed and take the tiny futon that usually belonged to Cody. Laura wouldn't agree to that and Carla felt out of her depth with this. Mostly because Laura seemed to be re- living a lot of painful things and questioning if she had reacted correctly. This was a triggering thing for Carla as her own experiences and feelings were not dis similar to what Laura was saying. Fair enough, the circumstances were very different, but the end result was the same. A damaged child who had then become a damaged adult who blamed herself for anything and everything. Carla's heart broke for Laura and indeed for anyone who had been hurt by those who were meant to care for them the most. Her head was pounding now and she felt sick in the very pit of her stomach.

Laura had decided a half- truth was better than a lie. She hadn't been through the trauma that Carla had, but she knew enough from supporting her all those years ago to make it seem that her father was more of a monster than he was. Some of the other things about her being punched by him were real, they had enabled her to continue crying and to keep Carla's attention for longer. They had been on the phone for two hours and she had heard the concern in Carla's voice; this had quelled her anger and her jealousy massively so she could now sleep; besides, Carla had invited her over tomorrow for a chat. If the lies got too much for her to keep track of, or the truth got too painful then Laura would insist that they get out in the car and do something. She didn't want to spend the day continuing a lie or re-living the painful truths that had really made her this way. Laura knew she wasn't a bad person. In fact, she knew she was a good person and that others just didn't get to know her enough before making up their minds.

Carla put the kettle on for another cup of cocoa. She wouldn't sleep now. Her head wouldn't switch off and the ghosts of her own past had really come out to play. No matter how Carla tried to divert her attention to something else she couldn't. In her head she was there again, helpless and bleeding. She was frightened now because she couldn't pull herself out of this world and had never been overtaken quite like this. She had known that she needed to be there for Laura. It had taken her years to speak out about this thing happening to her too and Carla needed to handle it carefully. It didn't matter that it had awoken something disturbing inside of her, she would never tell Laura this. This was a sisterhood, two people brought together by horrific acts, which made them have a deep understanding for one another. Carla wouldn't tell Laura how much it had intensified her own feelings of helpless despair and made her re-live her own trauma. She recognised that this wasn't about her, it was all about Laura, Carla had to hide her own feelings to be able to support her closest friend. She had eventually cried herself out and fallen asleep.

Laura woke up early, even though she hadn't set an alarm. She was excited. The time was only eight thirty and she knew the brats would now be in school for six glorious hours and Carla would be able to focus on her much more. She jumped out of bed with such exuberance that she heard a crack and realised she had broken a slat in her bed! It didn't matter. Laura had something to discuss with Carla. The boredom whilst she had been away had made Laura realise that she had to expand her circle and there were two ways she could do this.

The coffee flowed now, well for Carla at least, Laura sat there with an energy drink and the conversation was very different to the one the night before. Laura had more patience and the anger from the previous days had suddenly gone. She listened intently to the details of Carla's holiday and watched her gush with pride when she spoke of how Cody had learned to swim and how Ella had loved the petting zoo they had visited. Laura was always happy to listen when she had her own exciting news to share, indeed it had shocked even Laura. Carla was never the one in control of the conversation but, for once, Laura allowed her to be. The truth was, that for the first time Laura had realised how unjust her anger, tears and lies were yesterday and she wanted to make it up to Carla, even though she hadn't been aware of it at all. Once Carla had filled her in on the holiday, then Laura would surprise her with her own news.

"Sorry about yesterday duck, I just over thought things and it went from there. Anyway, while you were away I chatted quite a lot with a driver I work with and well, I really fancy him, he is called Glen and he's maybe not your type but he's certainly mine. He's been single for a little while too. Actually, if the truth be told this is the longest I have ever been single and well, I know it isn't long by your standards, but you know how I am."

Carla was a little surprised how fast this had happened, she had only been gone for a few days! Laura had been single for eighteen months or so and Carla worried that she was still a little vulnerable. The new love interest may be a decent guy and he might even be good for Laura but deep-down Carla was still worried. She didn't want to show it though because Laura seemed so happy, which was a huge contrast from the Laura that had been so broken last night. Smiling now, Carla and Laura continued the conversation in the kitchen as the kettle was put on. "Go on then Carla, I will partake in adulthood by means of a hot beverage!" This funny side of Laura was one that Carla loved dearly and the day flew by as they laughed and joked constantly just like old times.

After settling into bed that night Carla couldn't help but look up Glen on social media, she could find someone faster than the FBI when she wanted to. He had a teenage daughter from what the photos showed and she couldn't find anything that was a red flag, it was quite the opposite in fact and she now felt happy for her "big sis". After all, Carla had other friends and her children in her life and poor Laura only had her. She had been almost desperate to tell Laura about the surprise she had planned but she didn't want to steal her thunder, she would tell her on the day, which was "three sleeps" away. She smiled to herself, rested her head on the pillow and drifted off to sleep. At 3.30am Carla was awoken by a night terror and then sleep paralysis followed. She hated that, it felt like being suffocated by the dark. She knew this had only happened because of the things Laura had discussed. She was sure that if Laura knew that it would lead to this, she wouldn't have opened up to her but Carla would now never reveal the fact that even   years later she couldn't totally forget the horrors she had once suffered, no matter how much she wanted to. Carla didn't blame Laura for awakening the dormant memories her sub-conscious still held. She was just glad that she had been able to have a greater understanding of her best friend and "big sister" because of them.

Laura saw the caller i.d. show up on her mobile, it was Carla. It was 4pm on a Friday, she had told Laura she was going to take Cody for a ride and asked if Laura wanted to meet them there, Laura looked around the now empty office, she could get away right now, it seemed everyone else had abandoned their post. She sent a quick message to the drivers saying she would have her mobile on for two hours but was leaving the office. She grabbed her bag and left. The truth was that she liked the co-owners of the yard. They were fun and made her feel part of the stable yard, even though she only went every now and then. Cody was already on board a little grey pony when she got there. She didn't begrudge the children things like this; it was a part of both hers and Carla's childhood. As they were watching they heard the unmistakable sound of a horse box pulling in. It excited Laura, she always liked seeing what emerged from them. Was it a donkey? Was it a Shire horse? They would soon find out and no doubt meet the owner. "Can you two deal with that so I can carry on teaching Cody?" Called the yard owner, Lottie.

"Yes I am sure we will manage between us!" Carla replied.

Laura was used to Carla being super excited to meet new ponies but Carla was so enthusiastic that Laura worried that her mood may transfer to the new horse and then they may struggle to hold it. The woman in the box jumped out and greeted Carla in a casual manner. Laura had the feeling that they had met before, but this was hardly surprising, given that Carla had competed until her body gave up on her.

"Do you want us to help unload him Britt?" Carla asked. She kind of wanted to do it herself but then again he may be a bit flighty due to him being in a strange place and she was in enough pain as it was. She wanted to be well enough to be able to bring Ella here tomorrow, she had wanted to bring her along but Ella's lesson had landed today and was on a dressage yard ten miles away.

Laura saw a very shiny black pony with a white star on his forehead, he was stunning. Britt had handed the lead rope to Carla and Laura thought it was silly given that she was clearly much more balanced and well-built than Carla but Laura didn't feel she could say anything because she didn't know anyone there well enough. Britt handed a passport to Carla and still the penny hadn't dropped for Laura.

"Well…what do you think? Asked Carla. She genuinely wanted Laura's opinion because she had never gone solo when buying a horse before and Lottie was busy helping Cody down from the little pony. Carla looked at Laura who now had a puzzled look on her face." Is he for the riding school? because if he is he seems a little quick, if the way he came off the box is anything to go by." Laura always liked to be asked for her opinion on horses whether it was just in how striking she thought they were or whether it was more complex such as her going with someone to view a potential sale. She wasn't sure what this was right now, but she wondered if this horse belonged to Lottie or was this somehow connected to Carla. She seemed friendly with the woman who dropped the horse off and she referred to him as a "he" before he was even off the box.

Cody was done now and the grey pony was walking back to its friends in the field. Cody came running over to his mother and this startled the new pony. Laura was still trying to work out what the hell was going on when it all suddenly became clear.

"This is Beauty, Cody. He is yours and Ella's pony. Do you want to brush him? Then you can have a little walk on him as long as you let mummy lead you. Beauty is quite fast and he's only just got here hasn't he? and it's all new and scary to him but you can have a quick ride now and come back later and play while Ella has a ride on him, you must not tell her because it's a surprise."

Carla had found a small brush set for Cody in blue and one in pink for Ella. She couldn't wait to see Ella's face when she told her. As she turned to Laura, she thought she saw that she was looking really pissed off. As soon as Laura noticed her looking she totally changed her expression, but her voice didn't seem impressed as she made small talk with Lottie. Carla didn't want to call her out on it, not here anyway. It had put a dampener on her mood though and Carla found it difficult to hide her annoyance. Laura said she was meeting Glen and would drop them off at home but only if they were quick. Beauty was all tacked up now so it meant Cody could have a go on him before they untacked, flicked him off with a brush and then turned him out. Turning a new horse out with an established herd causes a great deal of excitement and comes with a slight risk of injury but he had only ever lived in a large mixed herd prior to this so Carla knew that he would be fine. He wasn't a young horse and she had paid peanuts for him. He was only £500 including an English Leather saddle that was worth around that anyway. He was 18 years old but Carla had wanted a horse that had been there and done that. She had ridden him herself and though he was forward, he also seemed sane.

"So basically, I am paying my taxes so that someone who can't work or maybe **won't** work can ride ponies all fucking day long. I can't even afford to loan a horse or pay for lessons Carla, yet you can buy your spoilt bastard children a pony! No of course I'm not pissed off, bad enough the tax payer is paying for your beloved crotch goblins, without them paying for you to play ponies all day long; as though there is nothing wrong with you! Look I just disagree with you living better than I can afford to when I work damn hard for my money, I just think it's unfair Carla. I am late now and need to get ready for my date, I will speak to you tomorrow ok?"

"You seem annoyed Laura, I thought you would be pleased, it means we can spend more time at the stable yard. I know he's too small for you to ride but Lottie has some lovely horses that you could book for a lesson or a hack and I will give you my lesson discount because I intend on teaching Ella and Cody myself. You see, with mates' rates on the livery this worked out cheaper than lessons. I came across beauty totally by accident when I visited Leah, you know, who we used to ride with when we were younger. There was a riding school across the road she said it was shutting down so we went to see if there was any cheap gear for sale that would fit either of the kids. I got talking to Britt who said the owner had gone into a nursing home and left her with the task of selling up, she wasn't concerned about money, she had enough to pay for her care, she just wanted to guarantee the horses went to good homes so Britt sold him for the cost of his tack only. He was £500 and I paid in installments if you must know!" Carla realised she had been ranting and didn't really want a row so she said goodbye to Laura and thanked her for the lift home and said she would speak to her soon. Carla's heart ached every bit as much as her body did now.

Laura was less upset now that she knew the pony was basically free but still felt that she was paying her taxes to support those who *wouldn't* or *couldn't* work and here was Carla, splashing out. When she had first seen Carla using a stick and looking so ill she had told her that she was glad that the Department of Work and Pensions had given her full Disability Allowance, after all she was born with a lifelong illness and it would never improve, she had worked, until her body completely gave in, leaving her with no option other than to claim benefits. It was something that Carla had always felt guilty about she had said but now Laura wasn't so sure. If she felt guilty surely she wouldn't allow herself and her brats this luxury lifestyle. These were things that Laura couldn't afford. The question was, was it that Carla really couldn't work? She didn't want to think badly of her little sister but there were a few times that Laura had felt this way. She dropped them both off at home where Ella was now waiting, having seen her mum and brother from Sylvia Wilson's window, next door. Laura tried to forget about the whole afternoon and get ready for her date with Glen. Things had been going really well whenever they spoke at work but this was only the second date. When she and Carla had spoken on the phone last night, Carla had told her to be sure that it wouldn't affect their working together before sleeping with him. Was Carla trying to control her? Could it be that Carla was jealous or was she looking out for her? The truth was that Laura didn't know what to believe about Carla anymore. She decided she wouldn't pick up the phone if and when Carla rang. Until Laura could work out how she felt and what the truth was; she decided the friendship would need to be on her terms from now on.

Bex thought that a change of scenery might help Carla, she had been through the mill lately and so had the children. She had been surprised that saving up for a pony hadn't lifted Carla's spirits though, after all, they had always helped her cope in worse situations than this. All she knew for sure was that when she and Carla had spoken this morning, Carla was like a kid at Christmas, she was so thrilled, but when she had called again after he had been delivered she was really quite down. The question was what had happened between then and now? Bex would get to the bottom of it when she picked them all up in a minute. She had already decided they could all stay at hers because she had a rare weekend off and she wanted to meet the famous Beauty.

Bex chatted to Carla, whilst being careful not to spoil the surprise for Ella. Cody had been told not to spoil the surprise for his sister. As it turned out now wasn't a good time to try and figure out what had gone on because the children were loud and excitable. Bex remembered what it was like to have a child of that age, though it now seemed so long ago. In the end the children were telling Bex about their lovely little holiday. Bex wondered why she was driving her Porsche down a dirt track; sure, she could afford to have it valeted but she was thinking she should have used the works estate car instead. Then again she looked at Carla who was clearly in pain and she was sure the heated seats would be benefiting her right now. Bex really was excited, Ella had been a part time carer to her mother for over a year and she really did deserve this little pony. It was always nice to share in Carla's family joys. Carla deserved for every day to be this perfect and Bex would make sure no one could spoil this weekend for them.

"Oh, mummy look! There is a horse here I haven't met before, can I go ask Auntie Lottie if I can pet it, I bet it's one for the riding school"

Carla nodded, Cody was in the hay store now jumping from bale to bale with Cooper, the Labrador. Lottie's lab was as bonkers as Cody and they often played with one another. Carla had told Lottie earlier that she would need Beauty bringing in and that she got to be the one to give the good news to Ella when she arrived. Carla and Bex had hung back slightly so that they didn't give anything away but it's good that they weren't too far away as even Carla hadn't expected that reaction. Ella had burst into tears and collapsed to the floor!

"Well, this isn't what I thought you would do. Are you happy darling? Mummy is so very proud of how helpful you are but you need to have fun as well, I know you love riding Grace and having dressage lessons on her but you're getting good now and this way you can ride two or three times a week, would you like that?"

"I am so happy mummy" said Ella, as she nuzzled into Beauty's neck. "Is he erm, what's the word…. broked in?"

"It is broken in and yeah sweetie he is, go and get your spare hat on I snook it here, it's on yours and Beauty's peg"

"Can I have a go mum?" Whined Cody.

"You can have a little one before we go, yes, but it's Ella's go first. I will shout you when it is your turn"

Ella got upon Beauty's back and gingerly asked him to walk on. He did so and didn't put a foot wrong and there were smiles all round. Cody had a walk over some trotting poles and then declared to everyone that Beauty did good "jumping" them. Carla felt her troubles literally melt away. Precious moments like this were what made her feel content and being at what had always been her "happy place" made her heart feel light, despite Laura's attitude to the situation.

The children ate their tea quickly and by 7pm their little eyelids were heavy. Bex carried them to bed and tucked them in. Carla was in the bath and Bex had told her there was no rush, she knew it was rare that her friend ever got a bath in peace and she wanted the three of them to feel rested, Bex hoped that Laura didn't spoil this weekend by phoning or texting at a rate that seemed almost impossible, it seemed to her that whenever Carla spent time with anyone else, or sometimes was just busy with her children, Laura would suddenly need her. She also hoped that she could maybe get Carla to shut off her phone even if only for tonight. Why couldn't Carla see it? Was Bex wrong though, maybe their friendship was intense on both sides. It wasn't the Carla she had come to know though. Carla was insecure, sure and who could blame her, but possessive, no way.

The Chinese food was as good as always and Carla had actually had a chance to kick back and relax which she was so grateful for. Bex really was so amazing with the children, they loved her, and she did them. She was patient with Cody and sarcastic yet fun with Ella. Carla loved staying here, it wasn't too often they could because Bex was basically the only veterinarian at her practice that could treat and diagnose her clients. Of course, she had a fabulous team of vets and nurses, but everything had to be overlooked and signed off by Bex. Carla realised as she was thinking of all this that even with such a demanding workload, a grown-up daughter of her own and the stress of owning her own business, Bex made time for Carla every week, rarely did she allow her work to stand in the way of their weekly ritual. Bex was a true and loyal friend, she had always felt that Laura was but now she felt unsure and for the first time since she had met Laura all those years ago their friendship seemed on shaky ground indeed.

Bex longed to broach the Laura issue with Carla, why was it that whenever she wanted to, she felt like she had to tread carefully? It took a lot to upset Carla, yes she could be oversensitive but somehow Bex felt this wouldn't be the case. Right, this was it, something needed saying, whether Carla took heed or not. Bex wouldn't be offended if she didn't, but she couldn't keep her mouth shut this time.

"So, I don't want to stress you out further but what has you on a downer? Anything between us is between us, you know that and you have every right to be happy. I know you feel you don't deserve anything nice because you didn't work for it; but anyone else born as disabled as you were would never have worked at all because they didn't actually have to. Yet you worked until doctors told you your body would break down irreparably if you didn't immediately stop. So, no matter what your negative inner voice is trying to convince you of, you shouldn't take notice of her, she's just a lying mother fucking bitch ok?"

Carla wouldn't usually want anyone to think badly of her other friends; but this time Laura had really got to her. She wasn't even sure what she felt about it. It was like she was a little bit mad, a little bit annoyed, a little bit defensive and a whole lot upset. Bex was a true friend to her and she owed her the truth. Although part of her knew what Bex would say. Carla decided that this time Laura had really hurt her which had never happened before, well not to this extent. Sure, she had made comments about any purchases Carla made of how "they look expensive shoes, lucky you!" in a sarcastic tone, but nothing this direct and mean.

"She said what?!" exclaimed Bex. She usually tried to give calm advice to Carla but this time she couldn't control her reaction. This wasn't a partner, this wasn't a blood relative this was someone who Carla had welcomed into her life, her home, her family. If Laura knew Carla half as well as she did then she would know how guilty spending any money on anything that was non-essential made Carla feel. Bex had been thrilled when Carla had said she wanted to buy this pony for her children. Bex had told her that if she couldn't afford him then she would happily foot the bill. Carla was a saver though and she always saved up initially for something for herself but then instead spent it on her children. Bex knew that while Carla couldn't ride (as trying this pony out put her in agony for over a week and she had only walked him round the block!) she would benefit from being on the yard with her friends, even if she was just brushing the odd pony and sitting and watching lessons. Why had

Laura not seen it this way? Didn't she realise that Carla had felt like ending her own life because she was in an undeniable amount of pain every day and she sat at home staring at the same four walls most of the week? This pony would offer her a lifeline, she could spend time with him while the children were at school, and Bex knew that being there at the place Carla had so many lovely memories with her friends would help massively. Friends who hadn't disappeared when her life had gotten tough, maybe Laura didn't want Carla to have friends. Bex didn't think Laura was as genuine as she seemed, she had already felt something had been "off" about how Laura had re-entered Carla's life only ever texting for the ten years prior even though she was at that time just down the road, with a car. Then out of the blue she had suddenly needed Carla, in the middle of the night and from there she had suddenly all the time in the world to spend with her and she claimed she had not one close friend aside from Carla? One of the beautiful things about Carla was how trusting she was of others, even though life had given her a million reasons to never trust another living soul. Bex knew that this often led to Carla being hurt or vulnerable and so she decided she would keep an extra close eye on Carla and her children from now on.

Carla almost felt she had betrayed Laura in some way by repeating what she had said. She knew of course that it would go no further, Bex had been her friend for years and had never repeated anything that they had discussed. Even so, the guilt she felt was deep, she didn't like it that Bex now wouldn't like Laura and it was all Carla's fault. Carla couldn't ignore the warning that Bex had given her though, she had reminded her that anyone who loved her would be happy that she at least had a release now, a way of dealing with the inner turmoil she felt at times. This little pony would give her a focus when her children were at school. Bex didn't resent the purchase and had reminded her that while Laura paid taxes, they would be nowhere near as high as the ones Bex paid out of her pocket and she was all for them getting Beauty. If he needed a vet then Bex had agreed to cover it so it wasn't a massive risk financially and if she one day couldn't afford the livery bill then Bex had said he could live on her land and they would buy a few more to keep him company. The truth was that Carla was grateful to Bex but preferred to pay her own way, even though now, she had been reminded by Laura that it was actually the taxpayers paying and this made Carla feel worthless and low. She decided to try and forget about the whole situation because it made her question buying Beauty, as well as her now questioning why Laura had been so mean, she had been all for the children having horse riding lessons, which cost almost what the grass livery did but this way the children could both ride a few times a week and Carla could teach them herself. Was it wrong to reward Ella for helping her when the pain meant she had to rest all day? No, Carla didn't feel it was. It wasn't ideal that at the tender age of nine Ella had to sometimes make either pot pasta for the three of them or cereal. She also had to help Carla in and out of the bath by offering her an arm to grab on to so that she could balance. Some of the time Carla and the children slept on the sofas if the pain meant that Carla couldn't walk the stairs. It was a big responsibility and this little pony would offer an outlet to Ella. The more she thought about this the more that Carla felt justified in her actions and the angrier she became about Laura's selfish outburst. Eventually she fell asleep in the enormous four poster bed in Bex's guest bedroom, and the only sounds that could be heard were those of restful breaths which came from her and Daisy dog.

Saturday was here at last, Bex lifted Cody into his child seat and did up his belt. Daisy clambered between the two child seats and Bex clicked her harness in, as Carla was clicking Ella's belt into place. It had surprised Bex when Carla had agreed to stay the whole weekend with her and she had opted to leave her phone switched off and on the bedside table in the guest bedroom, as Carla called it. Bex referred to that room as Carla's room and the bedroom next to that as the children's room, after all she had other guest rooms and a room with en-suite for her daughter, which was barely used now that she herself was an adult. Today would be everything for Carla that Friday should have been, Bex would make sure of that.

Carla saw Beauty coming to the gate and she offered him a sugar lump from her pocket. It would be a massive help to her if he could get into this habit so that she didn't need to trek down to the bottom of the field to collect him, her legs really weren't up to that anymore, she thought sadly. Soon she didn't have time to dwell though as Cooper came tearing along barking excitedly at Daisy, who spied him with caution before looking back to Carla. "Go on then you two, run along and play!" The dogs sped off through the open gate and began finding sticks on top of the muck heap, followed closely by Cody, who would play for hours with them both. Carla showed Ella which brush to use for Beauty's body and legs as his mane was too high for her to reach and Bex grabbed a tail brush.

Bex wondered if Carla had ever realised what a graceful and beautiful little rider her daughter had become, she found the two of them a joy to watch. How Carla had so effortlessly gone back into instructor mode, truly was a sight to behold; mother and daughter were both in their element and Beauty was every bit the dressage pony that Carla had said he was. Bex wouldn't allow Laura's negativity to ruin this for Carla and Ella.

"Mummy is it my turn now? I can jump the poles Ella; will you watch me? Mummy I want a turn now please"

Carla looked at Cody and was about to tell him to have a little patience when she suddenly burst out laughing, it was a good job she had found the waterproof all in one coat at britts closing down stall, Cody was covered almost head to toe in mud! Daisy was cleaner than Cody was! Carla was glad she had brought seat blankets for Bex car because there was no way that mucky pair would be allowed in otherwise. Bex was laughing now and asking Cody why he looked like a mud monster. She didn't even seem concerned by it! "Go to the toilets and wash your hands please Cody, then you can show Ella how good you are at jumping the poles and we can go faster if Bex holds the rope!"

Bex was smiling now and commented how Carla had misjudged her if she thought that she could go fast at her age, Beauty had better act his age and trot slowly or she and he would be falling out! Carla smirked and Bex realised it was the first time she had seen Carla smile like that since Laura had entered her life. Even before this incident, Carla spent almost as much time worrying about Laura as she did her children! Bex didn't know why it was that Laura had no family to be there for her, but she would do her best to find out.

Carla was feeling happier than she had in a long time, the children had spent all day giggling at Bex who was a bigger kid than either of them. They had played in the bath with some soap crayons and were now tucked up in their beds so that she and Bex could have some adult time. Bex had asked her to pick a film, Carla had picked one that she thought was a comedy only to find at the end that it wasn't and it had left Bex in floods of tears, claiming that she would now need an extra beer to get over it and that this was the last time she would ever allow Carla to pick a film, Carla was laughing so hard that Bex crowned her the ice queen which only made Carla laugh louder!

Bex would never let Carla pick the film again, comedy my arse, thought Bex and she sank her third beer. Bex opted for a film they had both seen a million times now, The Truman Show, at least no one died in the end in *this* film! As it played they talked about Bex latest case at work and about their lack of love lives and whether they should be worried about becoming old spinsters who end up with a million cats! Bex thought that it was likely they both would end up that way because neither she, nor Carla had the best taste in men. Both had ended up married to narcissists and could never really trust their own judgement in partners since. Alone was probably the safer option after all. Although Bex wanted to find out more about Laura, she didn't want to ruin what had been a stress-free weekend for Carla, who would be returning home after tea on Monday. It wasn't that she couldn't take them home before then, it was that if the children returned home tired then all Carla would have to do was put them to bed. Becky remembered her own daughter being young and how hard being a single parent with one child had been, never mind two! Carla was ill, mentally and physically at times and she wished that she could make her realise what an amazing mother she was, in spite of her difficulties.

Carla fell into the Egyptian cotton sheets and she thought to herself what an amazing weekend it had been, not because of the food or the luxurious bed but because of the company, it had been a perfect weekend, because she wasn't as tired and because she hadn't really given Laura a second thought. There was a pang of guilt now for feeling like Laura had made her stressed even though this was true, Laura seemed to get over her helpless state of mind before Carla had, maybe she just cycled through things quickly, maybe she

recovered as quickly as she unraveled. It was not the case for
Carla, she worried for Laura constantly and more so after each
episode. She felt guilty for switching her phone off, but it was late
now, she promised herself she would call Laura when she got home
on Monday.

Laura had enjoyed her date Friday night in fact it had continued into
Saturday morning, Carla had told her not to rush things but it was
clear to Laura that Carla was jealous, anyway this was the second
date, so she had held out longer than usual. What was so wrong in
wanting to feel loved? Glen had stayed Saturday until tea-time but
he had to work Sunday and so he had to drive back to his home
town an hour away. Almost as soon as he had left, Laura had felt
lonely so she texted Carla. "Sorry about last night, I have been
really stressed with work, I didn't mean to take it out on you sis, I
love you xx" Laura waited ten minutes, the text had still not been
read. She sent a voice note saying she wasn't mad anymore and
that she wanted to speak to her about something. It wasn't true but
Laura would think of something once she had heard back from
Carla. Two hours and several texts later there was still no word from
Carla. This was unheard of; Carla had always answered her texts
more or less straight away before. Laura knew that it was rare that
Carla could stay mad at anyone and besides, although she had
apologized she hadn't really said anything wrong, People on
benefits shouldn't be allowed to spend them on lavish things like
designer shoes or horses or tattoos or such things so, while she
could have worded it better she wasn't really in the wrong but to
stop it from ending the friendship she would be the bigger person
and apologize. It was unlikely that Carla would say sorry, so Laura
had no choice. By Sunday morning there was still no word from
Carla and every call Laura had made had gone straight to
answerphone, this was making Laura partly worried and partly angry
it was 11am, the brats would definitely be out of bed by now. She
decided that she would drive over if she hadn't heard back in the
next hour. An hour went by, Laura had called and texted every five
minutes and was seething mad by now. She got into her car and
headed over. She had rung the bell but there was no answer, was
Carla ignoring the door? Laura banged hard on the glass, knowing
Daisy would bark and then Carla would have to answer. There was
no barking, no sound of little beasts either. So, she headed to the
park realising they must be on a walk with Daisy. Nope, the field had

a few people on it with dogs but no spaniels. She was angry now and decided to drive to the stables, sure it was now just gone 1pm but it was on her way home. She was seething, less than a week in to having the geriatric pony and it was already infringing on the time Carla usually spent with her. Where else could she be, it's not like Carla could have gone for a run or a bike ride was it?!

Well that felt awkward, Lottie was mucking out and some other people were tacking their horses up and apparently Carla and the children weren't there, they had been at nine thirty in the morning and left before 11am according to Lottie. She wasn't worried now as clearly Carla was fine! She was an ignorant fucking bitch and now Laura was too mad to even keep calling her. Laura had no plans for Monday and she had the day off as it was a bank holiday so she would call her then.

Carla woke early on Monday and the children were still sleeping so she crept downstairs where Bex had already begun to grind coffee beans. Carla decided that while it was early she would switch on her phone and let Daisy out. Her phone pinged continually and there was a feeling of unease in the pit of her stomach now. What if something bad had happened to someone in her family and she had not had her phone on? As she was running through the possible scenarios in her head she realised she would have to let all the messages come through before she could check the missed call log.

"What's wrong with you, and why am I never this popular? Well, unless someone needs urgent surgery on their animal that is!"

"I don't know, oh my god, I have **eighty nine** missed calls and **twenty seven** messages and three voice notes all from Laura!"

"Over a two-day period, wow that's excessive to put it mildly!"

"That's just it Bex, these are all from late morning onwards yesterday. So, this is all in the space of a day and the last one was from two o clock this morning!"

Bex raised her eyebrow, one word that sprung to her mind was stalker. Did this happen, did women get stalked by other women? It wasn't something that Bex had ever thought about, but I guess there weren't only men that were stalkers, it's just that most cases are ex partners or obsessive men or women who find their victims attractive. This actually scared Bex a little, no one really knew much about Laura, even Carla wasn't sure why not a single family member or long-term friend had remained in Laura's life. Did anyone truly know Laura, what would she be capable of if she were pushed too far?

She glanced over at Carla as the coffee was brewing and she could immediately see the panic on her face, it was like this alone had aged her. Bex knew how she wanted to react and she wasn't usually so careful with her words but she knew that it would only add to Carla's stress levels so she decided for now to stay quiet, after all she had tried to warn Carla before because it was clear that the supposed "suicide attempt" was either a cry for help, or more than likely a ploy by Laura to instantly implant herself in Carla's life. Sure, Carla said that they had kept in contact but where was Laura three years ago when Carla had a full-on mental breakdown? Where was Laura when Carla had needed help planning her own 30th birthday? Where had Laura been for all these years? She had a car, and according to Carla, back then she had her own circle of friends so where were they now? Bex decided that this was where she should start.

All Carla could think about all day was Laura. The heavens had opened and the rain could be heard as it hit the roof of Bex's conservatory. Carla knew that if she told Bex she wanted to go home early she might be offended and she would know it was because Carla was worrying about Laura, so she decided to just call her.

"Put it on speakerphone, I know you trust her Carla; but I aren't too sure what to make of her. She knows how you have struggled with your mental and physical health and if you were up to working I would employ you myself; then you wouldn't feel bad for having bought the children a horse, you can't work which isn't your fault and their father won't give you a penny, so you have saved up. *You* deserve to have something to look forward to and so does *she*" Bex said nodding over at Ella.

Carla had never put anyone on speaker phone and she prided herself on never breaking a trust unless it was a life-or-death situation; but she had a nagging doubt in her mind because Carla knew she wasn't a good judge of character and if she didn't share these thoughts with anyone she would go around in circles within her own mind. She had never had a friend that was around as much as Laura was, but there were times, like now, where she felt nervous right in the pit of her stomach. Was she a bad friend? Laura seemed frantic in those messages; this might be why Carla felt nervous. The phone began to ring.

Finally, thought Laura as she saw her mobile screen light up, for all Carla knew she could be dead in a ditch somewhere! Tears welled in her eyes as Laura thought about this, she only had Carla, not being able to track her down had made her angry but it was a stark reminder that Carla clearly had others to spend her time with. Not sure what to do with this emotion she decided that the next time Carla called she would pick up the phone and let her hear how affected she was at being left all alone. She couldn't lose Carla; everyone she had ever loved had left her in one way or another. Visions of Amanda came into her head and this time the emotion was real, it was probably the only regret she ever had. Amanda had had it equally as hard as Laura had. There was no doubt in her mind that their mother should not have had children. Her father however could be lovely but was a complex man who often lost his temper. Laura took after him in that respect. She hadn't regretted walking away from that house, from **them**. Suddenly she was brought back from this emotional flashback by the shrill ring of her mobile phone. Reminded now that she and Carla were alike, they were bonded by their traumas, it actually made them closer than blood..

"I am so sorry Carla; I was worried about you and I have had the days from hell. I mean my date went ok but I almost crashed my car just now and I have been having visions where my child self was in the car with me and the blood and everything was so real and I know I shouldn't self-diagnose but I think that like you I might have p.t.s.d. Am I crazy? I am so sorry; I came to try and find you because I couldn't reach you, where are you? Shall I come and get you?"

Carla was absolutely racked with guilt now as it was clear from Laura's voice she was in a lot of distress and it was hard to even make out what she was saying through her tears. She looked over at Bex, who was now shrugging her shoulders. Carla mouthed "Shall I go?" and Bex had mouthed back "it's up to you." Carla had thought that Bex was right about Laura but then hearing her so vulnerable and seemingly desperate, Carla knew she had read this situation wrong and actually felt bad for being mad about what Laura had said to her. She could see Laura's point of view on her spending habits in a way and she knew that she would never again shut off her phone and be unreachable. Laura needed her and after ending the call she was about to gather up the children's things when Bex took them from her.

"It's alright Carla, leave the kids with me and I will bring them home at bedtime. I still aren't sure what to think but then you know her better than I do. I will open the gates so she can pull right up to the front door for you. It has been a lovely weekend and we shall do it again when my hectic work schedule allows. Be careful Carla, see you for a chat on Friday night for our usual take away."

After she had waved Carla off, Bex fired up her laptop. The children were busy playing in puddles in the garden and she could see them from where she sat. Now to input all she knew about Laura. Hmmm she knew her last "best friend" had been called Sarah Fraizer. There really couldn't be that many with that spelling from their little town. Social media made it so much easier to find people and for them to be contacted. Rebecca didn't have an Instagram account and she instead started up Facebook and began typing in the search bar.

Now back at her own house Carla took some of the ground coffee beans that Bex had given her and she made two coffees. Laura usually declined a hot drink instead opting for an energy drink, but she had accepted for a change. Carla was more than a little concerned now because she had never seen Laura like this, not even on the night when she had made an attempt on her own life! How had she failed to see that Laura being so nasty was her way of pushing Carla away? She was in fact completely unraveling. Poor Laura.

The tears were real, the upset was real. Laura felt like everything that had ever upset her, which she had kept inside was now erupting out of her and she could do nothing to stop it. She missed her sister Amanda, and if she could go back she would have done things differently because she needed her now. Her dad had been some-what of a bastard but then he was largely controlled by her tyrant of a mother. All the pain of her childhood could be denied no longer, she was her father's' only biological daughter and she was like him. Loyal, Sensitive and with a temper that would rival that of **The Hulk**, Laura knew that she felt differently to other people and that, like her father she was complex to say the very least.

Carla hugged Laura tightly, rubbing her back as she would a child. She recognised the way Laura felt, almost like a child trapped in an adult's body. Trapped. Carla had felt this, she had to fight the response this caused as her own emotions threatened to spill out. Now was no time to think of herself. Laura needed her, all of her; and this time Carla wouldn't fail her as she had done this weekend.

Laura was drained, she hadn't planned on this. Feeling this exposed. Laura had planned to lie, to fake some sort of crisis and now it had backfired. She didn't have post-traumatic stress disorder; she had seen how this made Carla react and she had planned on sort of faking it to a degree. So, it was true she had been physically and mentally abused as a child, she had been bullied because of her weight and yes her mind wondered to such times. Carla's didn't wonder back there; her mind was thrown back there, in a way. It was on the outside, as though her mind threw her body back there and she screamed and fought just the way she once had. It wasn't that Laura was faking because she really did feel these things so maybe she embellished a little but the rest was true.

Poor Laura, maybe she did have P.T.S.D. or maybe a multiple personality. That would explain how she could go from being so fun and calm to suddenly seeming like a different person. Carla had very little understanding of these mental health disorders there were so many possibilities. She felt that maybe it was time Laura was referred to the mental health unit itself, because the crisis team were useless to say the least. Carla could support Laura but she needed professional help as well.

"Laura I am so sorry I went off the grid, I thought you were working all weekend and if I recall you had a date on Friday night? You haven't mentioned that or we can keep talking through things if you prefer? I think you might have P.T.S.D. or a mental health disorder why don't you do a self-referral or I can do it if you want? I will listen all day long Laura but although I understand some of the things you went through, I aren't qualified and I sometimes worry I am out of my depth."

"I know what you mean and it can't just be depression surely can it? I have night terrors and all I can think about is Amanda. She went through some of what I did and I was forced to watch my mother kick the living shit out of her. But they still loved her and she isn't even my dad's biological child. Some of it makes no sense, but. I miss her" The quivering of Laura's voice happened as soon as she mentioned Amanda and she had to catch herself before she said too much.

"Well, you should write to her or contact her on social media! I am sure whatever was said between you can be put right. After all, you are actual sisters! Maybe I could find her on Facebook and send her a private message if you don't want to do it yourself?"

Laura wiped her eyes on her hoodie sleeve and seemed to cheer up at the prospect of Carla contacting her big sister on her behalf and after grabbing another coffee, Carla set to work sending Amanda a private message. Carla was good with words and truly believed that this would be an easy fix, only time would tell of course.

Bex had finally found Sarah, who had instantly responded and had gone on to explain why she and Laura were no longer speaking. She said that they used to go to the same stables. At the time Sarah had got her own horse and a small pony for the then little Andrea, her daughter. She hadn't had a row with Laura or anything but Laura had bounded up to her and loudly accused her of telling people that Laura had attempted suicide. This had been around seven years ago and Sarah stated that she had never said a word to anyone but that a week later when she couldn't contact Laura she had confided in Elaine that she was worried about her but not why. Sarah told Bex that this wasn't the first time Laura had done something like this and that she felt that no matter how nice she was to Laura, their friendship would never survive because of Laura's jealous nature and her unpredictable temper. Sarah had finally stepped away when Laura had given her little choice. She had threatened Sarah in the end saying she would" run her over as if she were a speed bump and that if it wasn't enough to end her then she would reverse back over her until her pitiful existence was no more!" Wow, this wasn't what Bex had been expecting at all. Sarah had seemed genuine though and it made Bex want to find out more about Laura but it would have to wait and she would have to tread extremely carefully. She didn't want to repeat what Sarah had said, the poor woman had clearly been afraid of Laura finding out.

Bex shut the laptop lid and rubbed her temples, she had thanked Sarah for the information and returned her attention to the children who were playing happily in the puddles that always formed on the patio. She smiled as she was reminded of how children could find fun in even the smallest of things. They really were sweet little things. How could Laura refer to them as spoilt bastards or crotch goblins? Thank goodness Laura hasn't had any herself, Bex thought. Right, what to feed these little humans, she must have some Quorn nuggets somewhere in her large chest freezer.

Carla felt better now that she had done something to help Laura. She had carefully worded the message so that Amanda wouldn't feel she was taking sides or sticking her nose in. There hadn't been any reply and the message had remained unread, but Laura had said her sister was rarely on social media so her getting the message might take a while. Even if she did read it Amanda may not respond at all, Carla didn't know any specifics as to why the pair of them fell out. Laura had said that the day she had fallen out with her parents Amanda had been there and Laura had said some things which she now regretted. Carla knew how much tempers could flare between families. Deep down though, she could see that whatever Laura had said, she regretted it now and the memory of that row was affecting her best friend badly.

Laura wanted to change the subject, she knew her sister wouldn't reply, and besides, some of the things she had said and done to Amanda over the years were just too much, thought Laura wistfully. It wouldn't do her any good to dwell and she changed the subject quickly now and gave Carla the juicy details of her date. At least with Glen, things were going well. Laura didn't do well on her own and she had stayed single after her bitter break up with Byron. He had caused her to have a mental episode and she had been carted off to the Psych ward while he had watched and told them they should never let her out! She would never let anyone do her wrong like he had. She had told Carla all about it when they had had one of their many heart to hearts. No one else knew the things that Carla did and Laura didn't want to lose her. She had meant the things she had said but just because she didn't like the children or didn't like how Carla spent her money, that didn't mean that Laura wanted to call time on their friendship. Carla knew that when Laura and Byron had split up, her parents had taken **his** side. He had almost broken her and she had no choice but to end things because he wouldn't change. Everything was always her fault according to him. The final blow where her parents were concerned was knowing that they still visited him, still walked **her** dogs. They were her babies but with nowhere to go and with her working full time she couldn't take them. She had been at the end of her tether then and had to be wrestled to the floor which took a squad of burly policemen. She had been in her pajamas and they had chased her down the street in full view of the neighbours. He was a narcissist as far as Laura was concerned. She had only been kept overnight and then discharged with promises of the crisis team following up. A week after this the police came and confiscated her guns. She had known this was coming and had sold some of them. (In the U.K. if you have a mental health crisis then your gun license is revoked as it's a worry that you may use one to cause yourself or others harm) She wished that she had wasted a slug in Byron but it would have been too obvious. Carla had said that she understood but she didn't. No-one had taken her dogs from her, so, she had been battered a few times by her ex, she hadn't lost her hobby, her dogs, her home and then been betrayed by her own family had she! Laura suddenly realised she was feeling angry again and Carla was looking at her expectantly. "Sorry duck, what were we saying? I keep having these moments where I lose focus and it's like what you said, it's like the past is playing in my head."

Carla was now concerned as she had witnessed Laura zone out completely and have a look of anger on her face without saying a word. Was this what a flashback looked like externally? Carla had only seen her own internally and had never met anyone else who had them. A bad childhood and a worse marriage had caused hers. It wasn't impossible that the same thing had caused Laura to have them too, and Carla was now surer than ever that Laura needed help but she wouldn't hear of it. How awful Carla felt knowing she had put Laura on speaker phone and allowed Bex to hear. They had spent all afternoon chatting and it was now 7pm. The children were still not home and Carla texted Bex to see when she was returning them.

"Right then sis, I will be off I have taken up enough of your time and the little darlings will be home soon to keep you busy. Sorry about all that earlier, I don't know what came over me. She leaned over to hug Carla and for the first time it wasn't awkward.

Carla was so pleased she had been able to help in some small way and she would always be there for her sister from now on. The guilt was less now, but she did still have that unsettled feeling inside, and she was sure that when she spoke to Bex and explained she would be feeling exactly the same, about Laura. How wrong they had both been about her. The guilt was still there in the very pit of Carla's stomach. Her heart felt heavy as a rock now and Carla hoped that she would wake up tomorrow and feel better but deep down she knew she wouldn't until she had made amends for thinking the way she had about her best friend. Carla felt like no friend at all right this moment.

Bex put the sleeping children in her car without waking them, she knew that she would have to carry them up the stairs and hopefully they stayed asleep. She was hoping she could share what she had found with Carla. As soon as the children were in bed Carla made Bex a drink and she was about to share with Bex how wrong they had both been but first Bex wanted to discuss something.

"She said what? I don't know that I believe that Laura would just turn on someone without just cause, I mean I know she did me. I know now she had a lot of tension built up over some things similar to mine. She also misses her sister Amanda and she was in a right state about it, honestly Bex I know you're suspicious and I appreciate you looking out for me but I don't think I will ever be taken in by someone again."

Bex shouldn't have let Laura have the opportunity to get her (no doubt fictional) version of whatever crisis across to Carla; who was so soft that Laura had somehow not only been forgiven for the awful things she had said but Carla was now worried more than ever about her. It was impossible to get her to see the wood from the trees now. Bex decided that she would have to keep a close eye on Carla, while also trying to find out more about Laura. This time though she would have to gather enough proof that Laura wasn't the person she made herself out to be. With work still pretty hectic she was worried that she wouldn't be able to find enough out, something was amiss where Laura was concerned and Bex was worried for Carla's safety. Sarah had asked that Bex didn't let Laura know what she had said. Was she scared of her or was she hoping to make up with Laura? Bex didn't know but it could be both couldn't it? If Sarah made friends with Laura she could keep an eye on her and maybe she wouldn't fear her. No, this was crazy talk, she had been over thinking it. Bex would get to the bottom of it one way or another.

Carla was exhausted and decided that tomorrow she would check on her inbox because watching it wouldn't make Amanda reply any faster.

The weeks wore on and with them came the summer months, Carla loved spending her time outdoors with the children, just the three of them. They rarely seemed to get time alone at the weekends because although Laura was still seeing Glen he often worked then and she now spent Saturday at the stables and Sunday at Carla's house. Carla still spent Friday evenings with Bex, who seemed to have finally stopped reading too much into what Laura said or did. In fact, she no longer mentioned her and Carla only mentioned her in passing.

Bex no longer commented on things relating to Laura but you can bet that every tiny tidbit of information she heard, she stored. Literally. She stored it electronically and also in a notebook titled patient files. She didn't know why she had done this but she was worried for Carla and this way if anything happened there would be proof of what -if anything- she found on Laura White. Lately Carla had mentioned that Laura and her boyfriend Glen had a speedy wedding booked. She shared her worry at how quickly things had moved, before chastising herself by saying

"Well, we both did the same so I guess we shouldn't judge" Bex smirked

"Yes we did and what a brilliant success it was…oh no wait that must have been some beggar else who lived happily ever after cos we married utter arseholes and were only happy ever after once we got rid of them!"

Both Bex and Carla were in fits of giggles while discussing their ex-husbands' shortcomings and doing ridiculous impressions of them. At times like these Carla realised that when she was with Bex they always ended up laughing. This didn't mean there was never sadness shared between them but that after the sadness they always ended up laughing. Now and again both at the stables with her other friends and here with Bex, Carla compared how she felt and while she never said it aloud she had to admit that around Laura, even though there was laughter she always felt like she was treading on eggshells. There was always a worry inside her that was there whenever Laura was, or Carla was losing sleep because she was worried about Laura. Deep down she hoped that once Glen and Laura were married she wouldn't worry about her so much. Even thinking like this made her feel guilty, it wasn't that Carla was selfish but the responsibility of being Laura's only friend was a heavy burden at times and had led to Carla having crippling anxiety.

It hadn't escaped her notice at the stables that her time was dominated by Laura, despite other people trying to befriend Laura and involving her in everything. It was almost smothering at times and she didn't try to even interact with the children here. Laura knew how to groom and tack up but all she really did was sit and watch, often distracting Carla who was trying to teach Ella how to look after Beauty. When she thought like this Carla often wondered if she was being too harsh on Laura. Could she do anything to distance herself just a little at the stables? It seemed that others left Laura and Carla to it and given that Laura needed more friends she thought it may help her if she interacted with others. Laura was funny, like really funny and she was able to ride horses and these were two really easy ways to interact with the other adults. It was almost like Laura didn't **want** other friends. Carla decided it was best to not over think this and to go with the flow. Laura did seem less stressed and her mental health was better so for the time being Carla would have to wait and see what the future brought. The wedding was only a month away now and then Laura would actually be moving an hour's drive away. It was both something to look forward to and a worry for Carla, while she did at times feel smothered by Laura, she wasn't going to be a short journey away if something happened while Glen wasn't there. Carla's mind went back to the night she had first laid eyes on Laura after a ten-year break. The image almost haunted her and this was probably why Carla worried so much about her unbiological sister.

Laura had seen how Carla had just picked up where she left off with Lottie and the gang at the stables. It had gotten her thinking. She had only Glen's family coming to the registry office and it would sure look odd. No one to even give her away on her own wedding day, it wasn't like her father could, not unless a miracle had happened. It was then that Laura decided she would have to swallow her pride and apologize to a few people. If she didn't what would people think of her? No one gets to her age and only has one friend. Sure, she had acquaintances but that wouldn't cut it. With Glen busy in the kitchen, she took a deep breath, a huge gulp of red wine and she picked up her mobile.

It was almost dinner time and yet that was the last thing on Carla's mind. She had to decide upon wearing the only thing that didn't look like a tent, she and Ella had spent all morning trying things on, Cody hadn't been invited to the big day, Laura had said it would be boring for him and well Carla had to agree so he was going to be staying with Bex for the day. With only one week to go Carla was wondering if she should offer to do a hen party but aside from Sarah, Sarah's mother Betty and Andrea who was now around the age of fourteen who else could she even invite? She hadn't known that Sarah was back on the scene until now, she would never mention to Sarah what Bex had told her and she hadn't mentioned it to Laura. She was pleased she hadn't now, otherwise they may not have been able to make up. Carla was sure that their falling out was a case of Chinese whispers or maybe Laura's paranoia because she was always worried about what people knew about her, but even Carla had to admit that the threats Laura had made were bad. She was just about to text Laura with the start of a one-week countdown when her phone rang.

"Hello Future Mrs. Wade ho….. Laura, what's wrong, slow down, no, no don't come here you can't drive in this state I shall come to you, where are you? The police station, Why? Stay where you are I will see if my next-door neighbour can have the children and then I shall get a cab.

Sat in the reception area of the police station Carla caught sight of a poster about where to turn if you are the victim of domestic abuse and she could have wept, Glen and Laura had seemed so happy and so in love and yet, if she had heard Laura correctly, Glen had headbutted her. Laura hadn't given her the impression that this had been going on, that said, Carla knew that there was a certain shame with admitting that your relationship is a sham where one person controls another with their fists. It isn't easy to admit because you love the person. Laura had never taken any flack from anyone in her adult life as far as Carla knew. So hopefully this was the first and the last time that Glen ever laid a hand on her.

Laura hadn't even left the police station when she typed the Facebook post. She didn't know why but putting things out there made her feel better.   "Well kids, the wedding is off because the bastard headbutted me!" There were already supportive messages coming in and all of her fake ass Facebook friends had begun sad facing the status. None of them really knew her. Some were people who she had met through online groups for different mental health disorders. Laura had joined at a time when she felt her symptoms matched their disorders and some of the people had added her as a friend when she had posted on them to ask questions. It didn't bother her that they hadn't met at all. The others were work colleagues from one time or another or people she had met briefly through other people. Their comments didn't matter to her, what mattered was that Sarah had seen it, as had Andrea and some of the drivers from her work, which ensured that Glen's closest work friends had seen it. She felt like jumping up and punching the air. He was still locked in the cells and by the time he would be released everyone he knew would know what he had done, she had tagged him in the post to make sure of this.

Carla had made sure Laura had driven slowly home, she couldn't believe that the police had allowed her to drive herself to the station after being headbutted, she could have concussion for all they knew! Laura had refused to go get checked out at accident and emergency though so they took that to mean that she was ok. As she poured the tea she reminded herself not to bombard Laura with questions, she was sure to be in shock the poor little love.

"Sorry about this duck, it came out of the blue really, it actually happened last night but I didn't want to wake you because it was early hours of the morning by the time the old bill showed up and anyway they arrested him and told me to go and make a formal statement when I was fit to drive. We had both been drinking and well you know how I get when I have had a few, so I am getting loud and he suddenly tells me to shut the hell up and I got argumentative then and next thing I know I am seeing stars and I had pissed myself. So, I dialled 999 and they took him away and the rest you know."

"Had he done…you know…this sort of thing before?"

"Carla do you really think I would have put up with it if he had done it before? No chance. I have never been afraid of anyone in the whole of my adult life, but I must have been, I mean I pissed myself through the fear and shock of it all and now I really don't know what to do. I mean I did make a Facebook post about calling the wedding off but we shall see what his lordship says when he gets out of the chokey." She laughed as she said this. The truth was that she didn't even know what Glen could remember about last night, it really depended upon whether he took responsibility or not because there was no way in hell she would marry him if he blamed her, she had been there before and never again would she be blamed for just about everything.

Carla didn't find this funny and she didn't fully understand how Laura could make a joke at such a time. She had let what Laura said about her not putting up with it go because she likely hadn't meant to be so careless with her wording. Laura didn't know what being beaten to a pulp was like on a daily basis and how breaking free of the coercive control isn't always as simple as it seems. Carla knew that Laura must be feeling all over the place and that as long as she had known her, Laura always dealt with emotional situations using humour. Carla didn't want her best friend to marry a monster. She hadn't even met Glen; they had had a brief conversation over the phone once when Laura had gotten drunk and called Carla. Glen had been laughing, he had seemed so easy going and he had found it funny that Laura was so drunk. He had sounded sober though. He was clearly a different person when he was drunk. Carla passed the tea to Laura and sat beside her. Carla placed her hand on Laura's shoulder as a sign of affection. It caught Laura by surprise and Carla could have kicked herself for doing it. Suddenly Laura grabbed Carla and hugged her, then came the tears. Carla had tried to hold hers back, this wasn't about her but it brought back so many horrific memories and it took all of her inner strength to push away the flashback that was threatening to take over. She had to be strong for Laura. Carla hated that her post traumatic stress disorder had chosen now to come and join the party. Carla somehow managed to stay present and focused on Laura.

It had been so long since Laura had let someone in to this extent. Sure, she had cuddled with Glen, she had cuddled with other lovers too but this was different. This was her actually letting Carla see her vulnerabilities. This wasn't an act and it wasn't for attention this time. Laura didn't know what to do. If she was without Glen, then she was nothing. She wanted to get married, it was something she had witnessed many people do in her lifetime, hell even Carla had been married and that woman was a trainwreck really. Laura felt a stab of guilt for thinking about Carla this way but, put nicely she was complex and complicated and she had managed to bag herself a man at one point. He hadn't stayed the course though, but then, aside from her she didn't think anyone had. Laura was determined to get married now. She cast her mind back to the previous evening. She had goaded Glen; she had known that all along. No woman deserves what he did to her but she had left off a vital part of the story; she deeply hoped that Glen's memory would be clouded. He loved her, she loved him too and that should have been the end. She didn't love his dragon-faced, fat, lazy, mess of a daughter though. She was spoilt and Glen was always going round to his ex's house and topping up her gas and electric! Laura couldn't fathom why he did this. He paid maintenance, a big chunk of his wage each month actually. Laura had never met Glen's ex-wife. She wished the same could be said about the fat ugly kid; but deep down she knew, she would have to make an effort with Abigail, after all; if they married then Laura would be her stepmother. Even the name stuck in her throat. Maybe Carla could help with this; after all she had managed to love her beastly little brats and they were both ugly as sin, snotty as hell and just about as dull as you can get.

Carla felt relieved when she looked down to find both children asleep. She closed the book she had been reading and she tried to calm herself with classical music, which usually quietened her mind. It had been a long and stressful day. Laura had stayed for hours, until the police had called her that is. As soon as Glen was released, Laura had left, desperate to be with him. Carla reminded herself that it wasn't her place to judge. That had been her not so long ago. With that thought came the flashback she had been fighting all day. She had known it would be powerful because that was the price she paid for pushing it back. She hadn't had a choice; in all the years she had known Laura she had never seen her so exposed. She felt honoured that Laura had trusted her, she knew it was something that didn't come easily. She knew that whatever Laura decided, she would be there for her all the way.

Laura spoke to Glen in a soft tone, all the anger of the night before was gone now. She knew now that she had crossed the line; the truth was that Glen probably didn't want to headbutt her and had done so in self defence. Laura hadn't lied about wetting herself, she had been afraid, Laura had known that slating Abigail and her mother the way she had would likely anger Glen. She had then been filled with rage and had begun punching him and telling him his fat ugly kid needed a lot of make-up and a diet and that even then she would still resemble a troll. She had meant it. Just the thought of that cola guzzling, burger eating, spotty bitch made her angry. She knew now though that Glen would never side with her over his daughter. This revelation had surprised her because she knew mothers were meant to side with their sprogs but she had thought that fathers were different. After all, Alex had been made to walk away from Carla and wasn't interested in his kids now. She felt sorry for Alex, Carla had taken him to court and they had basically stripped him of his parental rights for a period of eight years! He could apply to the courts and appeal but she thought he probably didn't ever want to clap eyes on his ex-wife and who could blame him. She had only heard Carla's side of the story after all. Laura had agreed with Glen, he wanted her to get help; he had said her drinking was out of control and that although he had been wrong to headbutt her he had been backed into a corner and she was literally kicking the shit out of him.

Laura suddenly remembered assaulting Glen as her memory came back and she recalled kicking him in his privates and then punching him in the face. She had two black eyes and the bridge of her nose was sore but Glen was quite literally black and blue all over. Laura felt a pang of guilt. Usually when she reacted this way it was deserved, Glen hadn't really done anything wrong though and Laura realised that she had been drinking almost every night for months. She did need help. Laura thought it was probably wise to see a doctor as well; she should check her liver was okay and it was probably about time she found out what was wrong with her. Laura recognised that she didn't see things the way others did but she always assumed it was because they were in the wrong. They definitely were of course, but maybe the way she dealt with emotions wasn't the same as others. She had purchased a DSM-5. It had been easy to find on Amazon, she had assumed it would only be able to be purchased by psychiatrists, (It was what they used to diagnose mental health disorders) but that wasn't the case. She knew she had something wrong and thought it could be bipolar disorder, or one of a number of personality disorders and probably post-traumatic stress disorder. She had learnt enough about the last one just from seeing Carla and how she reacted and how she described it. Laura knew that having that book could also come in handy. She wanted to be special, if Carla was then surely she could be too. Why should Carla be diagnosed with interesting mental health disorders. Laura had only ever gotten one diagnosis, and it wasn't correct. Doctors don't know what they are talking about sometimes.

Carla was unsettled when Laura had told her that the wedding, which was now three days away, was on. Laura had also heard from Betty who had said she, Sarah and Andrea would attend and let bygones be bygones. Laura had sounded excited about it. She had told Carla it was her fault that Glen had hurt her, she had been violent first. This hadn't changed Carla's feelings about this relationship. There was violence on both sides, which in her mind was a recipe for disaster. She chastised herself almost as soon as she had thought this. Who was she to judge? It may have been a one off, they had both been intoxicated. Hopefully Laura would stick to her word and stop drinking. Did she really have an alcohol problem or was Glen gaslighting her? Carla didn't really know what to think anymore so she decided to just go with it and try to be happy for Laura. The relief that swept through her, when she had heard that Laura had Sarah back in her life now, made Carla realise that for the past few years; she had felt overwhelmed by the crippling amount of pressure, that all of Laura's mental health crises had put on her. Carla didn't even feel guilty for feeling this way.

Laura was surprisingly nervous as she linked arms with Betty. How she wished it could be her father giving her away. The thought made fresh tears spring to her eyes but she managed to fight them, with a deep breath she walked towards the man she had chosen to be her forever. She wasn't wearing white, but then she was anything but a typical bride. In her red polka dot dress and black stockings with a bow and a line all the way down the back she had chosen to wear black heels too. This was the most feminine she had ever been in her life, Laura loved how she looked today but she knew that come tomorrow the rugby shirt, jeans and trainers would be back. For today though she had grown her hair and she was actually looking forward to spending time with those she loved the most.

Carla hated that, today of all days she had woken in complete agony. This could be a fibro flare, but Carla knew it could be any one of the physical issues which blighted her life. Of course, she hadn't been one hundred percent truthful with Laura. She had only mentioned the two most obvious issues. The truth was that Carla's back was a complete mess. She had problems with the nerves, muscles, disks and bones. She never mentioned any of this to anyone. Today though the arthritis was bad and of course fibromyalgia had to join the party. She didn't want to turn up to her "sister's" wedding in the dreaded chair! She knew she had no choice though. Ella would have to push her because today she didn't have the strength in her arms to push herself. They had finally made it and luckily there was a ramp into the registry office.

Laura suddenly got the giggles; she knew it was nerves but she was trying her best to control it. Glen didn't help matters as he was now smirking at Laura. How would they get through their vows like this! The registrar began with the usual spiel and thankfully Laura's nerves had begun to subside. No-one said a word when asked if there was any lawful reason they couldn't marry, which is always a tense moment even when you know you're free to. Laura had done it, she had finally found a man who was willing to take her on, for better or for worse. She wanted to be a better person and she wanted to make Glen happy. She had been able to get on with Carla when she was fourteen. Carla was grown up then though, she had always had an old head on her shoulders. Abigail was really quite babyish, she still called Glen Daddy and she sucked her thumb religiously. Laura knew she had now inherited the fat, ugly kid. She called her this so often that at times, she had to remind herself not to do it when speaking to her drivers at work or when speaking to Glen. She was going to have to make the effort and Laura promised herself that she would, starting with this week.

Carla really got along with Sarah and Andrea, they had both shared a horse until the untimely death of their beloved "Panda." They had spoken so fondly of the years they spent loving him and it had reminded Carla of her own one-in-a-million horse. She couldn't offer for them to ride Beauty because he was too small, both Andrea and Sarah were tall. She did say if they ever wanted a pony pat they were very welcome. Carla wondered why Laura had chosen to believe rumours over Sarah. It was clear to her that the three of them loved Laura very much. Carla reminded herself that Laura was rather insecure. She had always thought people were talking about her or making fun of her, Laura's way of dealing with this was to make fun of herself. Carla wished that Laura could see herself through their eyes. She was lovely and when she cared for someone she did so deeply. She was hysterically funny. Carla was overwhelmed now thinking of how lucky she was to have Laura back in her life. The day came to an end and Carla was eager to get home. Bex would be coming over for a Chinese when she dropped Cody off.

Bex tried her best not to ask about the day too much, she didn't tell Carla that she had tracked down Laura's Aunt. Things weren't as they seemed at all. Bex wanted to but she knew that she needed to find out more. Talking to Laura's elderly Aunt had raised far more questions than it answered but if what she had been told was true then Laura wasn't just a pathological liar, she was downright dangerous. According to the aunt, Laura was very violent she had stabbed an ex-boyfriend, he had dropped the charges in the end because he just wanted Laura to leave him alone. That wasn't all, she had been physically abusive to her mother. This was why her father had beaten her. Of course, this was only one version which was why Bex needed to find out more. She was hopeful that, now that Laura and Glen were married, Laura might back off a little and she would be able to worry a little less about Carla. Cody had been asleep by the time she had arrived at Carla's, so Bex took him to bed and tucked him in. He had such an angelic little face, so much so that if she had never seen him throw a full-on tantrum, she would never have believed he could be a little devil, then again even Lucifer was an angel once upon a time. She had taken him to the zoo today and he was truly mesmerised by all of the animals. He had loved the petting zoo the most. Bex would take Ella out for the day another time. Every time she spent any time with Carla's children, she felt a pang of anger and wondered how Laura could be so nasty about them. Bex had enjoyed the day every bit as much as Cody had. It had reminded her of when her daughter Danielle was small. Bex now felt she had taken those years for granted. They were the hardest but also the most precious. At least she could hand Cody back and she sure would sleep tonight.

Carla was tired, the sort of tired that sleep wouldn't really help with. She had really enjoyed the day and then Bex had helped her into bed, and they had eaten Chinese. Carla didn't like to eat in bed, but the truth was that sometimes she didn't have a choice. She had come home to a letter which was good news, but it had made panic set in. She had been offered a three bedroomed bungalow. Not one of the tiny ones where you can't swing a cat. It was a big bungalow, and it wasn't in the council estate. It was one of only two which were owned by the housing association in the privately owned estate. Carla knew that she had landed on her feet. She had visited the property last month. It would need work but once she had got it decorated a room at a time, she was sure it would be beautiful. The problem was she was going to get the keys in a week, and she would then need to move out in a matter of days. Bex had had a beer to celebrate on Carla's behalf but then, any excuse for a beer was a good one according to Bex. Carla smiled suddenly remembering the drunken times that she and Bex used to have when they were young.

Bex looked at her diary hoping that she could take the time off to get Carla's stuff moved. She would do it after work if she had to, but she was mindful that this wouldn't be easy to do. Her daughter Danielle lived opposite the new bungalow and Bex knew she would help. Carla didn't really have any help by means of family. Her own family were very much of the opinion that you are an adult once you reach eighteen and so Carla had done everything for herself, now of course she couldn't any longer. Bex didn't know how Carla managed with the children the way she did. It always made her proud of how far she had come, alone, and with all the medical issues she had. Bex had been with Carla when she was given the crushing news of the M.R.I. results, Carla had said that she didn't want anyone else to know, she hadn't wanted pity. She remembered how Carla had joked about how she would happily let Bex turn her into the bionic woman, how Bex had wished that she could. Bex could probably move all of Carla's contents in one day. Carla was minimalist when it came to furniture and the like, which would be a blessing now. Carla was probably asleep now. Bex had helped her with her medication so she knew that the morphine which Carla only used on very bad days to top up the slow-release fentanyl patch, would have knocked her out, which was a good thing. It was rare to see Carla in that amount of pain because on days such as these she tended to shut herself away from people. This bungalow might make these days few and far between, Bex hoped so anyway.

Laura hadn't contacted Carla today, she had been shocked seeing her in a wheelchair, relying on Ella for every little task. It had angered Laura in a way as Sarah had not paid as much attention to her as she had hoped. Carla had gotten on with Sarah as though she had known her years. Laura hadn't got the gift of conversation in the way that Carla had. Laura didn't know if this was genuine, part of her understood this mystery illness and how it must impact her little "sis." But then she also wandered if indeed Carla deserved an academy award for her performance. It confused her so, that she decided to leave it a few days and concentrate on keeping her husband and his sprog happy. Laura knew she would enjoy the wildlife park whether the fat, ugly kid came or not.

Carla left a text for Laura; she was excited and scared about the move to the bungalow. She knew that once it was at least liveable it would have a massive impact and improve her health and indeed her mental state. She didn't want to call Laura as it was the first day of married life and she didn't want to intrude upon the pair of them. Carla vaguely remembered what it was like to be head over heels. The memory of herself and Alex in those early days was so blissful that she allowed herself to smile about it, for the first time since it had all come crashing down around her. Her thoughts were interrupted by Cody who had woken and was now pulling back the quilt and climbing into bed beside her. He put his arms around her neck and gave her the most gentle cuddle. The children seemed to know when Carla was in pain, and they were always best behaved when she needed them to be the most.

Laura had been awake for hours and yet, there was Glen, snoring away. She didn't want to wake him. They had consummated their marriage last night while they were both worse for wear, she didn't like sex as much as she had when she was younger. The thrill of it when she had first met Glen had gone now; in a way one-night stands were more of her thing because it was the thrill of the unknown. With Glen she knew what to expect, it was all over in half an hour or less sadly. She certainly hadn't married him for the sex. He was a good man though and he accepted her for who she was. She knew he wouldn't betray her as her fiancé had years ago. Nor would he want her carting off to the loony bin. Glen loved her, really loved her; exactly as she was. Laura knew she had landed lucky finding him. Unfortunately, though, to keep him she would have to keep his fat, ugly kid happy. She had made an effort yesterday and she had invited her to go to the local wildlife park with them both. Glen and Laura had both taken a week off from work but had decided that rather than going away they would go on a few days out. One of those days was to a distillery which was the only way Laura could guarantee that Abigail wouldn't be invited along. It annoyed her how much Abigail had got her father wrapped around her little finger. Laura's phone had gone off and she was hoping that it was Carla. A week off had seemed a good idea at the time, but now Laura wondered how she would fill the days. Glen would likely sleep until dinner on the days where they had nothing planned. Laura decided to go and see Carla, she would be awake by now so she would be at the stables or at home; probably the latter as she seemed in pain when Laura had seen her last. That's if she wasn't faking it for attention, even on Laura's wedding day it couldn't be all about her. Carla had turned up in a bloody spaz chariot! Laura didn't think a wheelchair was necessary, yes Carla was in pain but surely, she could have got a bus and walked across the road and back! Laura had forgotten about it until now and she decided she would check on Carla and see where she was. It was over an hour's drive away from Glen's house, but she had plenty of petrol and deep down she wanted to see if she could catch Carla out. If Carla was genuinely ill and having a flare up of whatever the hell was meant to be wrong with her, then Laura would be able to put the kettle on. She read the text. Ah so she's managed to get a bungalow then. Laura wasn't jealous. Sure, she herself would soon be moving into Glen's house fully. She hadn't wanted to because it was on a council estate and Laura felt they were beneath her. She had grown up on a housing estate close to the town centre, it had been rough and anything that wasn't nailed down was stolen. Since her early twenties she had always lived in small villages, often paying over the odds for the privilege.

Carla had heard the door, the problem was that she knew she couldn't get down the stairs, even with Daisy's help. She didn't like to send Ella to the door because she didn't want to put her in danger. She didn't know what to do for the best! "Ella, don't open the door or unlock it but can you go and ask who it is for me please?" Carla could hear only muffled voices and she heard the door open. "It's only me! Guess you're stopping up there, I better make you a grown-up drink and get you to the window somehow for a ciggy cos I am guessing you're stressed enough to want one?"

Carla was at first relieved and then a little confused. Laura was on honeymoon right now and yet, here she was. Not one to look a gift horse in the mouth Carla said yes to both the coffee and the cigarette. Carla didn't smoke often at all maybe three or four per year if that. She had given up when Alex had left, funnily enough she wasn't stressed out daily, without him throwing his weight around. The idea of moving house within the next week when she felt this bad made Carla want to cry. Deep down she knew that moving would mean that even when she was like this, she would be able to get to her own front room, unlike now. But she still knew that it was likely going to be expensive and impossible. She couldn't top up with morphine now not with the children awake. They didn't mind playing upstairs, this meant that Carla could hear them. She couldn't even paint on a smile today; she managed a weak one as Laura came through the door with her tray in hand. If anyone could make her laugh though, it was Laura.

Laura had somehow convinced herself over the past few years or so that Carla was on the swindle and that she did so because she couldn't be bothered to work for a living. Sure, Carla had used a walking stick and even a wheelchair, but deep-down Laura had felt that this was either in a bid for sympathy or to convince those around her that she was ill. Now though Laura was genuinely shocked and concerned. Carla hadn't known she was coming so this couldn't have been an act. Laura did, every now and then genuinely feel for others. A lot of the time she feigned emotions that she knew other people felt. Carla wasn't emotional often either though. The two of them had suffered traumatic experiences which they weren't at the time able to speak of. This was why Laura felt bonded so fiercely to Carla. They hadn't been able to show emotion as children. They were taught that to cry was weak and unacceptable and this meant that even though the two were out of danger and now adults, they still were often unable to cry, Laura could turn the tears on, only when she felt angry.

Carla was glad that Laura had dropped in on her. She had needed to see a friendly face and even though she knew that Laura wouldn't help with the children in any way, it was still good to know that for those few hours at least, there was another adult in the house. The only drawback to this was that Laura always stayed for hours and hours on end and Carla was tired and was struggling to hide her pain to the extent that she usually did.

Laura had spent all night questioning herself about Carla, it had become almost obsessive, and Laura knew that it had, but she hadn't been able to stop herself this time. Years back when she had had a therapist, he had told her how to shut down this type of behaviour, the problem was that Laura didn't always *want* to stop obsessing. Her mind wondered back to then. Doctor Steel had been good at his job, everything he had said about Laura had rung true. She did struggle in relationships, she worried about being abandoned, yet she often abandoned others. Her own parents had completely checked out when it came to her. They had chosen Kevin over her and before this, they had chosen Amanda. Laura did worry a lot about what people thought of her. The people closest to her mattered the most. Doctor Steel had understood her, in a way that no other person had. She had loved the attention he gave to her during those sessions. She began to think he was different with her, that he must be similar to her for him to have such a good understanding. He may have had a wedding ring on his finger, but it was crystal clear that he fancied her. Men usually did, hell he probably even loved her. Laura didn't mind sleeping with married men, she had done so many times before. She had only agreed to go to therapy in a bid to save her job. Losing her temper had almost cost her, her livelihood and reputation. Sure, transport planning isn't a highly skilled job, but she had certificates and she had worked hard to get this far. She shouldn't have threatened to ring Simon's scrawny neck and she shouldn't have picked him up off the floor. The truth was that Laura's temper usually frightened her much more than it did anyone else. She had been ordered to find a good therapist and attend anger management sessions by her employer. The anger management was utter rubbish, she had to stand up and say, "My name is Laura and I have an anger issue." It was so cliché. The group was full of woman beaters and psychopaths. Laura didn't belong here; she had been pushed to react. She had found Doctor Steel's information on the G. P's noticeboard at her surgery. She had thought it would probably be a waste of time, but Doctor Steel had sensed that she had inner turmoil and was struggling with something. He hadn't ever been able to drag it out of her because some of the things that Laura struggled with made her feel too ashamed to ever speak of them. Laura had attended well over the minimum number of sessions, and she recalled with much emotion how difficult that last session had been. She didn't want to leave; those sessions were her lifeline. She hadn't any real friends to speak of back then, and though she had paid for his time, Doctor Steel had said that the diagnosis she had now received meant that she needed someone who specialised in the disorder she suffered from. The anger and bitterness had bubbled deep within her soul, and she had loved Doctor Steel. She had opened up to him and yet, he had chosen to abandon her. It felt like such a personal attack, how dare he tell her to go elsewhere? She did not want to go to another shrink. She did not want to talk to anyone at all after Doctor Steel had uttered those final words. Her anger was untamed then,

Laura had vowed that day that Doctor Steel had sealed his own fate and never again would he build up a patient only to tear them down. Even the memory of this made Laura's blood boil and she threw back a handful of herbal sleep aid pills in the hope that sleeping would quell her demons. She saw him now, in her mind's eye. The blood had spilled out onto the carpet of Doctor Steel's office and Laura had fled the scene in the hope that she could slip out of there as stealthily as she had entered. She had known by now that the receptionist left early on a Friday afternoon. Good old Doctor Steel, letting her go like the saint he was she thought, sarcastically.

Carla had barely slept. She was no longer worried about moving, Laura had told her it was not an issue because she and Glen would handle it all. So, all Carla had to do was box up all that she wanted and needed and cull anything that was broken or old. There was no way she could fit everything from a three bedroomed house into a three bedroomed bungalow. She was so glad that Bex and Danielle had come to help her. Time was something that wasn't on their side. Glen would be here in a day to move the boxes to the bungalow. Carla was very stressed at this point but she was so grateful for Bex and Danielle and so she knew that she had to keep going, even though the pain was almost making her gag.

Bex was trying to sneak a glance at Carla, sure, she had said she was fine, but her face told Bex otherwise. In a way Carla's independence was commendable but, in another sense, it was downright frustrating. Bex couldn't help but smile though; Carla was probably the most stubborn woman on the planet. Doctors had warned her that her fragile body was breaking down and she was essentially facing a life in a wheelchair, and still Carla wouldn't quit. If she became unable to care for herself then Bex had decided she would have to come and live with her, kids a dog, a pony and all. Bex hadn't said this out loud to Carla; right now, she knew that Carla wouldn't thank her for her pity. Until it actually happened, Carla was so sure she would prove doctors wrong and Bex didn't want to sound like she had no faith in her.

The alarm sounded at 8am and it was moving day, so Carla dragged herself out of bed. She had been awake for the past hour and nervous butterflies sat in the pit of her stomach. Laura and Glen would be here at nine and then chaos would likely ensue. How sorry she would be to bid goodbye to the neighbours who had been a part of her daily life for the past seven and a half years. They had seen her through every bruise, every row, and her eventual heartbreak. Her elderly neighbour had advised her on how to keep the children from running wild and how to toughen up a bit. Her other neighbour had been there to run to when Alex's temper had got the better of him, she had helped Carla put money aside in the hope that she would leave him. Jo had even sent her husband round to mow the lawn and, the truth was that there were no neighbours quite like them. Carla couldn't do a lot now as yesterday had played havoc with her body but everything she didn't need was now in the skip that was at the top of her driveway. She had asked her current neighbours to keep the drive and the road clear for a period of two hours and she was hopeful that with the help of Laura, Glen, Bex, Dannielle and her neighbour Jo she would be moved in no time.

Laura didn't like any sort of physical duty but even she knew that Carla couldn't do this alone. Glen was a proper work horse when it came to manual labour, so he was sure to make light work of a poxy house move.

Bex hadn't met Laura up close before and she didn't really want to but at least she could get a proper feel for her. With Sarah shutting down on her Bex had struggled to find out a lot. Sarah had said she would never forgive Laura, but Bex knew that Laura seemed to have a way of controlling most situations and that she was skilled when it came to manipulation. Bex passed a few boxes to Glen and realised that Laura had decided to make everyone a cup of tea, which would no doubt be needed but not before the work was done. Danielle made sure that Carla was okay and was busy organising all the boxes marked "living room" at the door for Glen to load onto the truck.

Within two hours Carla was standing in her empty hallway with Daisy at her feet. This house had been a home for Alex, herself and Ella and shortly after moving in Cody had arrived. Her memories triggered a terrible post-traumatic episode as Carla relived the day that Alex had almost killed her and Ella. Alex had texted saying he wanted immediate access to his children, she had said that she wasn't home. Carla had sat in silence behind her front door, not even daring to breathe; her children had been sleeping in their beds. Carla had expected that he would come, she expected that he would be angry. Carla had known deep down that Alex didn't love his children. It was almost like the novelty had worn off. Sure, he had been a good father to Ella for two years, but Cody had been planned and then Alex had a change of heart. She shuddered as this different flashback took hold. Daisy was pawing at her now, but Carla was completely engulfed within herself and was at the mercy of her unpredictable memory. Alex had tried to strangle Carla and he had choked her until she actually passed out. This was when he had known Cody was the boy he had been hoping for. Carla should have ran then, but she was completely controlled to the point where, when he had been arrested for battery, she wouldn't make a statement. The Crown Prosecution Service had decided not to prosecute on that occasion and Carla had been so relieved. She knew that if Alex had copped another charge for domestic violence, they would have thrown the book at him. He would have made her pay and at this point she didn't know if it would cost her, her life. The flashbacks kept coming and Carla was thrown into panic as her mind became like a rabbit hole, which eventually led her to **that** day. The day that the nightmare had reached a dramatic climax and the day her marriage had ended.

Carla had arranged for a friend of hers to come and change all the locks. She loved Alex and a big part of her couldn't imagine how she would cope as a single parent. She was afraid of making decisions now, which was a complete contrast to the person she had been when she and Alex had first met. Carla had been strong, determined and fiercely independent. She didn't know where that person had gone but Carla knew she needed to find her again. Alex had put his key in the lock that day. Carla had sought the help of the local Womens 'Aid but she hadn't wanted to go into a refuge. She knew Alex had a temper and she knew she was afraid for her life, but she wouldn't admit to herself that it was that serious. The woman in charge at Womens' Aid was called Flora and she was truly good at her job. She had made Carla feel at ease, while also being firm about what needed to happen. She had wanted to move Carla and the children immediately; but Carla had been adamant that although she was sporting many bruises, she didn't feel Alex would hurt the children, nor would he pose a risk to her life. Carla allowed Flora to get an emergency restraining order. Flora had made sure that Carla had sent a text out to Alex telling him he needed to find immediate accommodation. She had then provided Carla with a new sim card so that Alex could not contact her. The restraining order was temporary, but Carla had been assured that at the end of the two weeks, a permanent one would be made.

Laura was exhausted. Carla had barely lifted a finger, claiming to be in too much pain. Bex and Dannielle had believed her and had been making her sit down a lot. Laura was slightly pissed off with Carla. Not only had she not helped to move things; all she had really done was pointed to bags and boxes, but the sprogs were at the new house and Laura had been saddled with them while Bex went to find out where Carla and Daisy the dog were.

Bex could see Carla crumpled up against the front door she was hugging her knees and screaming. Daisy was barking, no doubt trying to bring Carla out of her episode; but it was clear from Carla's desperate cries that she was trapped in a world where she no longer belonged; if Bex could take all of those memories away, she would do it in a heartbeat. She had known the first time she had witnessed them that it was likely some form of P.T.S.D. She had sat in the doctor's office with Carla, when the G.P. had said that Carla had to go to a psychiatrist for an official diagnosis. Laura had insisted on taking Carla. Bex didn't trust Laura at all. She had tried to warm to her, today when they had met for the first time in person but she still didn't trust her and Bex was still busy trying to track down any family or friends who would fill in all of the blanks where Laura's past was concerned. Carla couldn't see what Bex did, she was too close to Laura to see the wood from the trees. Bex honestly worried for Carla's safety. She had witnessed only that day how false Laura was with the children. It was like she was repulsed by them both. More so with Cody, Laura was definitely false with him at best. Bex had actually left Dannielle with them so that she could watch both the children *and* Laura. She now tried hammering on the door to startle Carla out of the flashback, deep down she had known it was futile, but Bex felt so useless. She decided to see if the back door was open; though a lot of the time Carla would lock herself in; so that she felt safe.

Carla tried telling herself it was okay, that it was just a flashback but sometimes the grounding techniques just didn't work. Alex had broken down the door now. He didn't just look angry, he looked totally unhinged. Carla had seen him angry; she had feared for her life before, but she had never seen the look in his eyes that she did now, and she didn't know what to do for the best. Ella was on the landing now rubbing her eyes, as she stared at the broken front door. Carla looked up at her and tried to speak but she didn't know what she *could* say. Ella may have only been small, but she was far more advanced than her years and Carla knew that telling her to go back to bed, probably wouldn't have made a difference. Carla found she could barely speak, and her words came out in a whisper. "It's okay baby, Daddy and Mummy just need to talk"

With her back to Alex, Carla had given him an even bigger advantage. She had felt her hair being yanked back with such force that she was sure she would have whiplash. Now Alex had soaked her almost head to foot, while she desperately tried to free herself from his grip. All the while, Ella was watching, glued to the spot by fear. Ella knew that smell, she had smelled it before when Daddy had set a fire outside to burn rubbish. She looked down on her mother and father in absolute horror as she saw him reach into his pocket and Ella suddenly wasn't afraid; she knew it was up to her to save mummy this time.

Alex hadn't planned on the children being awake. He had intended to use his key and slip in the house undetected by them and slit their mother's throat with the cut-throat razor in his pocket. He would then take **HIS** kids and he would burn down the house which is why he carried the petrol. Now though he didn't want to give Carla a quick death, why should he? She had not only got a court order against him, but she had changed the locks, like she thought she could erase him so easily. Alex wanted to hear her screams as she burnt to death. She was **his** wife and this way, she always would be. Now though Ella was pulling at his trouser leg trying to prize him from her mother. Alex took the cut throat out now and released a terrified Carla.

Ella was crying now as the cut-throat was pressed firmly against her neck. Alex was crying too. He was telling Carla that if he had to die then Ella was coming with him. Carla could have grabbed her phone and called the police, but she knew deep down that she and Ella would be dead before they arrived. Carla spoke with a calmness that she certainly didn't feel. It was as if she knew that her only way of getting Ella out of this alive was to stop Alex from feeling trapped by the decisions he had made. She didn't really care if he lived or died now. She had spent the whole day crying about the thought of living without him but now she couldn't have cared less if he had taken his own life, but there was no way in hell that he was taking Ella with him. She had barely begun to live for goodness' sake. She knew that although she seemed to be getting somewhere all it would take was one wrong word and the three of them would be dead!

"I have nothing to live for, my own mother is ashamed of me and doesn't want to know. I know I messed up breaking my sister's arm last year, but it was a year ago and I am still her son. A mother's love is unconditional, isn't it?" Carla had to tread so carefully, and she chose her words with a great deal of thought. She knew it must sound genuine and believable and honestly, she wished she could sit and sob but there was no time for that. She was already having to try and ignore Cody's cries and hope that he managed to get back to sleep. He was two years old and still in a cot thankfully. While the commotion had probably awoken him, Carla knew he was safer where he was. Alex hadn't bonded with him so he would think nothing of taking him from Carla. She looked into Alex's eyes, and she saw that he was genuinely emotional now. He was a Jekyll and Hyde and could flip easily from one mood to the next.

"Well, my love for our children is unconditional; but you know that my own mother doesn't feel that way about me. They are the ones who aren't wired up right. We are probably a little messed up because of them, aren't we?" She had taken a few steps towards him now and was almost in touching distance of Ella, but she knew better than to try and grab her. Alex was tall at six foot five inches. He towered above Carla and looked a giant next to Ella's tiny frame.

"You can get your life back on track Alex, you have other family, and you have the children to live for. They both love you and they need their Daddy in their lives. Ella is worried about you, probably more than she is for herself right now. You can leave now and walk away from this but if you carry through with your threat and can't bring yourself to go through with taking your own life and you are caught, they will probably lock you up for life. With your previous record it could well be indefinite. Please listen to me Alex. I was wrong to get the court order. I thought your mother would put you up, I never wanted to leave you homeless or feeling so desperate that you might do something like this. I think we should talk, properly over a cup of tea. I really want to resolve this like adults."

Alex had suddenly loosened his grip on Ella, and she fell into Carla's arms, sobbing uncontrollably. Carla knew now that she should have taken the advice Flora had given her and moved away from the area. She asked Alex if it was ok for her to try and soothe Cody who was screaming at the top of his lungs now. Carla allowed herself to relax if only for a second and she had put the children's' channel on for Cody and his crying had now begun to quieten to a murmur. Carla hadn't wanted to pick him up as she was still soaked in petrol. She left his room and went to put on the kettle. She grabbed another top from her room. Her priority wasn't Alex; but to keep her family safe she knew she had to manage this situation and she didn't feel she could do it alone. She picked up her phone and sent a message to her then mother-in-law; it simply said: "Come to mine, come alone and be calm as one wrong move and Alex may do something he will live to regret!"

Alex's head was spinning with the emotional roller coaster he had been on in the past half an hour, it was hardly surprising. He had loved Carla, he always would. She made him crazy, and he wished he could be like other blokes; he wished she didn't push his buttons. Sure, other men didn't think the way that he did, and they probably didn't feel as he did either. Without Carla he wasn't Alex, she had replaced his addiction; more powerful than any drug, Alex couldn't get enough of her. He loved her with the same intense passion as he hated her with. Alex was complex; he knew that, but then so was Carla.

Sat at the kitchen table now, Carla and Alex would have looked like a normal married couple to someone passing by. Carla was so good at looking calm and controlled when really, she was panicking, her mind was now scrambled and erratic. Alex had begun having this effect upon her way before any violence ensued. She had to sound convincing; their lives depended upon it. She could have called the police before heading downstairs and the truth was that she hadn't known why she didn't do that. Any sane person would have, but deep-down Carla had known that this was the most dangerous Alex had ever been. Sure, there were times he had taken scissors to her throat and where he had warned her that he would slit her throat as she slept. She would try to stay awake all night, just in case. But one thing Alex had never done was threaten the lives of their children. He hadn't mentioned Cody, but he had no bond with his son so if he was thinking of taking the lives of Carla and Ella, then there was no way he would leave Cody unscathed. "How much access do you want?" Carla asked, her voice low but steady. She glanced up from her coffee cup as she spoke. How she had wished that she drank alcohol right now because she could do with a whiskey on the rocks. Alex didn't look as scary now as he had done ten minutes ago; he looked defeated. One wrong move though and it could all change. His mother would be on her way so, Carla hoped beyond hope that Elsie would see that Alex was a man on the edge and that his behaviour wasn't a result of Carla "pushing his buttons," which was how Elsie had always viewed it. As it happened when she had arrived, Elsie had seen her son clearly for the first time in her life. Ella had come flying down the stairs when she had heard her Nanna's voice and she wasn't crying but her eyes were wide, and she looked utterly petrified. Elsie had taken over the situation. She remained calm as she spoke to Alex, and Carla knew she was safe or soon would be anyway. As she closed the door behind Elsie and Alex, she was struggling to keep a lid on her emotions, but she hadn't allowed herself to cry until an exhausted Ella had fallen asleep. She picked up her mobile and called the police. She had promised she wouldn't, but if she didn't do something now then she knew this could continue to happen and next time Carla might not be able to talk Alex round as she had done tonight. She wept hysterically as she retold the whole story to the two police women. They promised her that it would be dealt with efficiently. Carla wanted to guarantee their safety and only this course of action would do that. Still, she had gone to court hoping that instead of punishment her then husband would receive the help he needed. The problem was that though Alex had once remarked that he would never be happy in his love life because he had, and would always, hit women; Carla had known he wouldn't openly admit that to anyone else, let alone someone in a position of authority. The judge had taken into consideration the fact that Alex had a long history of violence against women, and in general, he had also read the letter that Carla had written, requesting that her soon to be ex-husband get help rather than punishment. The letter had only made things worse. She was still under Alex's control, and the letter had proved this so the judge remarked that he hoped she and her family would in time heal from the trauma caused by Alex. He gave him eight years and had banned him from any form of contact with Carla, Ella, Cody and their wider family. Carla was both relieved and gutted. She started divorce proceedings soon after.

Carla hadn't felt herself slump to the floor; she must have ended up there in the throes of the flashback. Her eyes were swollen now and her cheeks, tear stained. How she wished she didn't have to relive these things. It made her feel weak; like she had failed in some way because she could never be over the things that had scarred her emotionally. That was the nature of complex P.T.S.D. She wouldn't have gotten the diagnosis if it wasn't for Laura and Bex. How amazing her non biological sister had been to her. Carla now had renewed hope that this house move would help her mentally as well as physically. Daisy was still beside her having licked Carla's face to try and help her come around. She could hear Bex now and hauled herself up onto her feet.

As Carla locked the door for the final time Bex had linked her arm through to support her friend. She knew from the look on Carla's face that she had relived some horror in that flashback. As a close friend Bex often found it hard knowing all that she knew about Carla; bastard men! Bex was sure neither she nor Carla would trust one again! Carla stood back to take one last look at the house which held so many memories. The good ones were really good, but the bad ones were truly the stuff of nightmares. Alex could be out soon as he was three years into his sentence. Bex wished that there wasn't this stupid rule in the U.K. that if a prisoner behaved "inside," they could reduce the sentence by half and sometimes less. Alex was a horrible monster of a man on the outside. Behind bars though, Alex was a model citizen, and though Bex didn't think it was fair that the law here worked this way she knew, as she was sure Carla did that in the not-too-distant future Alex would be a free man, free to terrorise her once more. Bex only hope was that Carla went ahead and got a non-contact order. This is a legal document which, while not stripping a parent completely of their parental rights, limits the parent to postal only contact, usually only at Christmas and on the child's birthday. Any other contact with the ex-spouse would be banned. Bex thought that this might help Carla to move on. She hadn't so far. While Bex knew her friend no longer pined for Alex, him coming out was bound to make her anxious. At least for now he wouldn't know where she was.

Carla couldn't believe that she was in her new home with all her things within a matter of hours. She had unboxed the living room things and later on she was planning on unboxing the kitchen things. This new home would offer her and the children the new start they deserved. Laura and Glen had been amazing, and she knew she owed them far more than a hundred cigarettes, which was all the payment that Laura had said she would accept. Bex and Dannielle wouldn't accept a thing. Carla felt so indebted to them all that she could have wept. She probably would have done were it not for the fact that Carla knew Laura would tell her she wasn't to let a single drop come from her eyes. Although she wouldn't word it so politely, Carla smiled as she realised that she knew her best friend so well that she could almost hear what Laura's response would be.

Laura was exhausted, well aware that this wasn't how people were meant to spend paid holiday days. She knew that she had to help Carla though. It wouldn't have looked very good if Bex had been made to drive all Carla's stuff here in her tiny works van. Not when Laura and Glen had a large haulage truck. It had only taken two hours to move everything. Laura had made a swift exit because the local pub would be open when Glen and Laura got back to the disgusting council estate. She hated this place and why they had rented a house in the roughest area in a twenty-mile radius was beyond her. Surely with two wages coming in they could afford a nicer house than **this.** His lordship wouldn't hear a bar of it though. This shit hole of a town was where he had grown up and with the ridiculous amount of maintenance he paid, they simply couldn't afford the houses that Laura had in mind. It still stung that Glen's ex-wife lived in luxury and had never worked a day in her life. Laura and Glen worked damn hard for their money, and they were stuck in a rough as fuck part of Norwich while the smack rat ex-wife and the Carla's of this world sat on their arses and lived like kings. She was angry now and Glen spied her questioningly. Laura could never tell him how she truly felt, she knew he would stick up for Lisa, though after what she knew of his ex-wife, Laura couldn't understand his loyalty to her. Lisa had, had countless affairs and smoked weed and god knows what else on a daily basis while also claiming to be too "depressed" to work. Finally, Lisa had filed for divorce citing unreasonable behaviour on Glen's part. Glen wasn't upset by this, and he was no doubt happy to be shot of Lisa but because they had the fat, ugly kid, Lisa was entitled to a large part of Glen's salary. Wouldn't you think that was enough? It clearly wasn't though, as Glen was always topping up the electric or getting them shopping. Laura would put her foot down about this just as soon as the honeymoon period was over. The smack rat's days of sponging from him were numbered. Of course, Laura couldn't prove it was smack that Lisa was using but she was gaunt and stick thin and Glen clearly liked a woman with thick thighs and curves and he got this when he met Laura. Lisa and her fat, ugly kid would be getting cut off sooner rather than later. For now, though, Laura fixed a smile on her face and made small talk all the way back to Norwich with Glen.

Carla woke up later than usual and had to rush around so the children wouldn't be late to school. It might make better sense to move them to the village school soon. She didn't drive and though the towns school was only ten minutes in the opposite direction, she knew that the village school (which she would now be in the catchment area of) had a better Ofsted report. She made a mental note to enquire about this when she got home from dropping the children off. Carla felt like she was in a hotel when she had got up that morning. She felt better already for not having to walk down the stairs that morning and she was in a better mood mentally. Laura had texted last night to check in on her and Carla had told her that she was so grateful for Glen and Laura's help, and she had meant it. This bungalow was beyond her wildest dreams. The housing association rented it out for well below the market value. It wasn't like their usual properties. With small enough gardens for Carla to do herself it boasted a private drive way; it really was ideal for what Carla needed. Daisy wouldn't mind a smaller garden; she was walked three times a day anyway. Though Carla couldn't walk much, she didn't need to as she had a ball lobber which sent the tennis ball miles away. This was the perfect game for Daisy who was every bit as neurotic as you would imagine a spaniel to be. Carla took Daisy with her on the school runs because this way she could kill two birds with one stone so to speak. How she loved the leisurely walk home, Daisy was a perfect pooch and she loved Carla with every fibre of her being. Carla often wished she had a partner, but she had been burned too many times and Daisy was so much easier than coping with a man. Carla was pretty sure she had forgotten what to do with one of those. Of course, she could always shack up with a woman, well she could if she was out of the closet; which of course she wasn't. People would refer to her as "greedy" if they knew she was bisexual. She had known that she was, from being fifteen years old. She had been with girls first then, but Carla had seen Laura taking the piss of one child who she had said was "definitely a butch lezza!" thinking back on it, Jade was only ten at the time, Laura had been a grown ass woman. Jade had left the riding school and not returned.   When Carla and Alex had got together, a small part of Carla had decided she wouldn't have to come out this way. She wasn't in denial at all it was merely that people presumed Carla was straight and she didn't tell anyone otherwise. Her old friend Ember had known but only because she had slept with Carla for a few years before Alex had come along. Carla knew even in her late teens that she could never "come out" to Laura. Laura made no bones about the fact that lesbians and gays annoyed her. She used bad homophobic slurs. She had once mentioned to Carla that a co-worker was "the biggest gay in the village" and that Laura had to leave work early "before she put the bender through the fucking window, without opening it first." Of course, it may be that Laura just didn't like **him,** but deep-down Carla knew that Laura wouldn't view her the same if she knew. As much as this saddened her, Carla wouldn't risk losing Laura so she would keep it to herself, Laura was worth the sacrifice.

Laura hadn't missed the "big gay fuck" that she worked with. Simon was as dramatic as you would expect a raging homosexual to be. Laura had almost thrown him into the stained-glass window of their big office block once. She had made an excuse that Carla had fallen and needed her, and she had then called Carla and begged her to call her work and verify her story. Carla hadn't wanted to lie, and Laura did feel bad asking her to, but it wasn't like Carla would ever meet these people and with Laura's past record she couldn't afford to lose her temper again. Don't get me wrong, the last work colleague that Laura had set upon wasn't LGBTQ+, she was a single mum who didn't have a clue how to run a transport office. Laura had wanted the job they had given to old. sad Susan. She had worked at the company far longer; hell, Laura had even put up with the old pervy bastard (who used to be in charge) slapping her arse. She thought that when he retired, he would put her forward as office manager, she had worked there for years and felt that the job should have been hers. Sad Susan (as Laura always called her) couldn't arrange a piss up in a brewery. It still irked Laura that she had to practically run the office for peanuts. Susan had left after a few not so gentle nudges from Laura. Laura had known it wouldn't take much to get rid of her and it's not like she had bullied Susan. She had worked for a smaller company before this, but she had been sacked for losing her temper. This wasn't something that Laura ever divulged; in fact, it wasn't mentioned on her cv because she was all too aware that this didn't paint her in the best light. It wasn't that Laura couldn't work with others; it was that this office was full of idle people who didn't want to pull their weight. Laura hated the lazy, idle bastards. Her face was twisted once again, and Laura caught sight of this in the rear-view mirror. The traffic had come to a roaring halt and Laura hoped she wasn't late in. No one would say anything to her, she had been the boss since old sad Susan had gone on sick leave citing stress. Laura had smiled when the sick note had been emailed to her. She knew that Susan wouldn't be back. It was better that she leave of her own accord, Laura hadn't wanted things to turn ugly.

Bex hadn't known what to do about Laura. If she took her on, she might be forced to tell Carla what she knew, and Carla would wonder why she had kept digging. Bex only wanted to protect Carla. Laura would never be good for her. It had been clear to Bex when she had found out about the chequered work life Laura had led. Now though she still hadn't heard from Amanda and the aunt she had got in contact with had suddenly clammed up. Ivy, (Laura's great aunt) mentioned that Laura did have a mental health condition but the old dear couldn't be sure what it was. She had said that Laura had seen a shrink called Doctor Seal, was it? The poor old love said her memory wasn't what it used to be and Bex hadn't wanted to upset her. After this conversation dear old aunt Ivy had ceased replying. Bex didn't blame her, it was draining trying to find answers and Bex almost gave up until she had heard about the doctor. Bex had to get some sleep now as she had a double hip replacement on a geriatric terrier in the morning, and the hours had ticked by fast.

Carla had finally emptied the last box. She had got a decorator in, and half of the house was done. Her dear old neighbour had presented her with a cheque the week before Carla moved stating that she wanted to help in some small way. Carla had almost fallen down with the shock when she had seen the amount written. She begged Sylvia to take the money back, but she may as well be speaking Chinese for the good it would do. This money would pay for flooring for almost all of the house! Sylvia was a kind old soul who had come to treasure those beautiful children as much as she had their mother. Carla smiled as she remembered baking cakes and sending them next door. Sylvia had always been grateful for these small gestures and had often listened to Carla's woes without judgement. Carla accepted the money but insisted that Sylvia come for tea every month because Carla did not want to lose touch. Sylvia was like a mother figure for Carla, and it seemed the two of them needed one another. Sylvia's nest was empty now and she rarely saw her own son. Carla felt the familiar feeling of love swell in her chest and a tear snuck down her face. She hoped that the new neighbours would become as dear and as lovely as old Sylvia had, though Carla doubted this. For the first time since she had moved in, Carla felt gutted that her health had brought about this move. She was grateful, of course she was, but she knew that in time she wouldn't be as close to Sylvie as she once had been, and this fact deeply ached within her heart.

Bex was exhausted, she had meant to check in with Carla, but time had eluded her and now it was too late to call or text. She had wanted to see how things were going and it made Bex feel like a bad friend when the day was over, and she hadn't had the chance. Bex couldn't sleep, so she had decided to do a bit more digging and when she had, she only wanted to call Carla all the more. Where was Amanda? Why had she not responded to any of the messages that Bex had left? Sarah, Andrea and Betty and Sarah's son, Kaden, were all back in with Laura now, so it was unlikely that they would shed any light on the matter. What had Great Aunt Ivy said she thought Laura was diagnosed with? Bex fired up her laptop and grabbed the notebook from her shelf. It was a good idea to make notes, after all Bex needed some sort of record of all of this. She was now more sure than ever that foul play had been involved. Amanda wasn't online at all and though this could just mean that she no longer used her social media accounts it could also mean that Amanda didn't want to be found. Doctor Steel sadly, had been found, with a biro buried deep within his windpipe. He had been left to die and wasn't reported missing for three days because he sometimes slept at the office. The poor bloke had died from his injuries. The crime scene had been squeaky clean, and not a scrap of evidence had been found, that was, aside from a partial fingerprint on the biro. The problem was that it wasn't a match to anyone the police had on file. "The receptionist had said that she last saw the deceased at 1pm on the Friday, A police spokesperson said"

The newspaper had come in handy, but it didn't prove a thing. Bex felt dizzy, and her instincts told her that it couldn't be a coincidence, Laura's shrink had been found dead! Bex couldn't prove that the foul play involved Laura any more than the police could. All that was certain is that Doctor Steel hadn't made it home to his wife, and he never would. It was clear that he hadn't stabbed himself in the throat, but someone had. Bex would have to see if she could get any closer to the truth before she warned Carla, but would that come too late?

Laura still had nightmares pertaining to Doctor Steel, she had never seen so much blood, as she did that day. Her anger had truly overflowed, goodbyes were never her strong point. She had watched the light go out in his eyes. In one respect she hoped he would make it, but that was a lot of blood. In another respect, she didn't regret a single drop. She had trusted him, and he had thrown her back on the mental health scrap heap. He had met her demons and yet he left her to battle them alone. She had known they would finish him in the end. He hadn't a clue either, the poor sap. She wouldn't forget the look of shock on his face when she had rammed that biro into his neck. She hadn't made an appointment; in fact, she had been officially discharged from his care. She had made him pull up her file and she had read all his notes about her. Part of her wondered if she should make him change the diagnosis and delete the fact that Laura was reluctant to see another therapist. It wasn't a therapist she had needed according to his notes; She was a lost cause according to him. Doctor Steel had said he wasn't qualified to work with someone with the type of personality disorder that she had. Laura didn't like the diagnosis; she had looked up a few different ones in the DSM-5. Borderline personality disorder seemed to fit Laura, it fit her like a glove in fact, but good old Doctor Steel had other ideas. Possibly Narcissistic Personality Disorder, he had stated, matter of factly, though only a psychiatrist could diagnose that. Laura hadn't wanted to go down that avenue. She had made it clear where he could stick his ridiculous ideas! She felt the betrayal personally, Laura lay in the dark with her demons. They had robbed her of her future husband, she knew that Alistair loved her. Laura hadn't wanted to take Doctor Steel out; she had loved him; He couldn't say that he loved her of course but he had wanted to pass her care onto another doctor. Laura was sure that once he discharged her, he would take her out to dinner. He couldn't date her while he was treating her, but the little things he said and did told Laura that he liked her. "Take Care, Laura!" he would smile at the end of each session. "Don't forget to use the grounding technique I showed you if things get tough!" Alistair Steel was every bit a professional, he was as gorgeous as he was clever, and his pearly white teeth and trim waist made Laura's heart skip a beat. At least if she had a heart attack Laura would be in good hands. She was smiling now but Laura wouldn't be smiling for long. The memory was vivid now, she could almost smell the metallic odour coming from his corpse. Sure, she had ran from the building but even if someone had found him it would be too late. Indeed, Laura couldn't let him live, not after she had spilled her guts about what happened with her parents and Amanda. He knew too much, and as she lay in the dark Laura reminded herself that Doctor Steel's death was necessary; She had sat in silence as the light in his eyes faded. She couldn't allow herself to think about him, so Laura tried to put him to the back of her mind. Glen had started to snore; Laura held onto him for all she was worth. She was Mrs. Laura Wade now, she told herself. Laura White was as dead to her as Amanda and her parents were.

Carla hadn't heard from Laura all week and she now began to worry. Should she call? The texts had been read but she had received no reply. Was it a bit full on for her to call at nine in the morning on a Saturday? Laura hadn't said whether she had a riding lesson booked, nor had she asked Carla to book one. Laura had never offered to pay for them because she took Carla and the children places. Carla felt indebted to her and after all, Carla felt that Laura deserved to ride if she wanted to. Unlike her, Laura worked hard for her money. Besides, Carla didn't mind paying for Laura to join them, it would cost her the same amount in taxis. Laura wasn't visiting quite as often now and with fuel prices going through the roof; Carla understood that money doesn't grow on trees. Bex would be in theatre now until later on. She had cancelled last night because an emergency case had come in. It was exceedingly rare that Bex turned a client away; as long as they had the funds, (and sometimes even if they didn't) Bex would always be willing. Her passion for animals had never altered. Carla felt alone, all of a sudden. She didn't know her neighbours yet and she desperately missed her old neighbours. Carla dialled Laura's number and hoped that she would answer.

The screen lit up, Laura had been awake hours and was sat in the dimly lit old living room. Nicotine stained the walls and the ceiling, and the place needed a complete revamp if Laura was to stay there permanently. She only had her own flat until the end of the month, Carla's number showed, and for a minute Laura simply listened to it ring; unsure whether she could be bothered to answer. With a deep sigh she answered and opened another can of energy drink. Laura hadn't spoken to Carla; she hadn't got the will to, if she were being honest, but a small part of her loved the fact that Carla had seemed desperate to speak to Laura; she **needed** her. "Yes, I am up duck, what's the matter? I was going to come for a ride this morning anyway so I may as well pick you three up on route. Sorry I have been missing in action, I have worked a lot of hours since I went back to work as it's not like the biggest gay in the fucking village can pull his own weight. Ugh I can't wait until I retire, ha no I know, I have a while to go yet, we can't all be ladies of leisure." Even as she said it Laura felt like a raging bull. Carla was medically retired and would never work another day in her life, that bitch really did have it all. Laura hadn't meant to get angry and had said she would be setting off shortly, anything to get off the phone so she could vent her frustration. She wrote a note for Glen and left; Laura opened the door to her fiesta. Once inside the tears sprang to her eyes and Laura screamed and cried and hit the steering wheel with her fists. It wasn't fair that she had to live in a shitty old semi-detached house in the middle of fucking junkie-ville while the likes of Lisa and Carla lived in well to do areas of town. It wasn't right that those unwilling to work got everything they ever wanted, and Laura got the shitty end of the stick. She was driving now but was on auto pilot and before she had known it, she was on the motorway. Pull yourself together Laura, she told herself.

Carla helped Cody into his jogging suit. His beautiful locks covered his forehead and Carla made a mental note to take him and Ella for a trim over the next week or so. With winter fast approaching Carla had been looking online at electric scooters for both of the children. They were outdoorsy types, and she knew that they would appreciate such fun gifts. Money was tight and Carla had to make up for the fact that Alex wouldn't bother. He never had, though he had complained loudly about the non-contact order, the truth was that he didn't think of his children, even at Christmas, or on their birthdays. Alex thought only of one person: himself. Carla didn't mind, life was easier this way. Her children had never missed out on anything just because she was a single parent., if anything Carla had more money than when she had been married to Alex. He had dominated their finances and often spent all of the money on designer gear for himself. Sometimes he had spent the money before she had even paid the bills. It wasn't a problem for Alex, he knew his mother would bail them out, Elsie always had done. She was a lot of things; and she always put her own children ahead of her grandchildren, but she wouldn't leave them without anything. Carla felt so ashamed as she cast her mind back to then. When Alex left it had transpired that he hadn't paid Elsie a penny towards the washer she had purchased for them on credit and yet as far as Carla had known it was almost paid off. She had given Alex the money religiously, he had probably bought drugs with it, knowing him! It had been a long road to recover from Alex's wrath. Sometimes Carla wondered if she had recovered. Would she ever be able to get over what he had done? Fire was something that Carla feared now. Alex had done that to her. The smell of petrol was something that Carla used to like, though she didn't these days. Alex could be a free man soon. Did he still hate her? Carla wanted to find out and she had come close to writing to Alex in prison but when it came to it, she couldn't find the words to say to him. The Alex that she had fallen for had been false, he didn't exist, so the shell of a man in that prison cell wasn't *her* Alex.

Laura had collected Carla and the little crotch goblins and driven them to the stables in near silence. She would drag this out until Carla asked her what was wrong and then Laura would tell Carla how depressed she felt. It wasn't a lie; married life was mundane, and she was feeling down. The housing situation was less than ideal and with Christmas soon looming Laura would have to witness the fat, goofy kid getting hundreds of pounds worth of shit, that she neither needed, nor deserved. The very thought of this made Laura's blood boil. It was a good job that the doctor had put her on beta blockers now. Between Carla and Lisa, they were testing Laura's patience. She loved Carla though, so it was complicated where she was concerned. Laura hinted at the fact that she had forgotten her purse because she had no intention of paying for her ride. After all, the money Carla had rolling in was paid for using her taxes. She had saved them a cab fare anyway so it was the least that Carla could do. Now as the children had exited the car and ran down the lane to the riding school Laura had Carla to herself. Tears formed in her eyes, and she didn't wipe them away, instead she let them flow and Carla looked full of concern, which only spurred Laura on.

Carla suddenly felt like the worst friend in the world! How was it that she hadn't seen this coming? Poor Laura always seemed to try and handle things alone and Carla hadn't even realised her best friend had been feeling so bad. Christmas wouldn't be the same this year. Laura would be spending it with her new husband and stepdaughter. Carla thought this might do Laura good. Sure, she and Glen's teenage daughter didn't get on, but people are usually more tolerant during the festive season. The wind whipped around Carla's legs now and she shivered as she pulled the coat around her. Laura didn't seem to feel the cold today although she had mentioned once how it made the metal work in her back hurt a lot more. Laura had never fully got over her accident. It showed sometimes when she rode. There were times that she hesitated before kicking the horse on to canter. Carla had noticed this, but she didn't like to ever remind Laura of the day she almost died. There was never any pressure for Laura to ride, let alone to canter but Carla thought it was possible that Laura put pressure on herself. Not one to be outdone by anyone, Laura wasn't going to show any sort of weakness to Carla's closest friends.

Laura dried her eyes; the horses were just ahead now and being tacked up in preparation for their lesson. Carla had herself began to ride, she would never jump, and she never rode anything that was sharp, naughty or fast. She never knew whether riding was the right thing for her to do; but until her body told her otherwise, she would ride once a week. It was likely that, this was enabling Carla to lose weight and to be more mobile than she had ever been before in autumn. This was the one day a week she and the children got out of the house and did something as a family. Cody didn't always ride and though his spot had been booked, it didn't matter if he changed his mind. Tiny would be tacked up just in case. If he didn't ride, she would happily trot off in search of hay in the field.   Ella had come off the lead rein now and had cantered a few times. She was visibly frightened when beauty surged off initially but half the way round Ella would regain her composure. Jumping was something that beauty excelled at. When Ella was ready to jump, they would make quite the team and Carla couldn't wait. Show jumping was in her past now. Her back was unable to take the impact of jumping and it didn't bother Carla anymore. Her time in the ring was done but Ella's was just beginning, by the time show season came around next year they would both be ready for it.

Bex finished up in theatre and left her team to close up. She was beyond tired now and she knew that she must get home and sleep to feel refreshed enough to build a prosthetic limb for an unfortunate cat that had been hit by a car the day before. Bex knew though that with everything she had on her mind, sleep was not likely to come easily. So, she decided to drive home and see what Great Aunt Ivy had to say. The old lady seemed to look forward to Bex' calls now and she was making headway into finding out who Laura Wade really was. Small snippets of info would be given without the old darling even realising it. Bex had already searched the news archives for any suspicious events relating to a doctor. She had recoiled in shock when she read about Doctor Steel. But Bex couldn't find a link to Laura. Data protection would stand in the way of her finding out no doubt. Say she was right, and Laura had been his patient like the little old dear had said, why would Laura want him dead? The crime scene, though gory, was pretty clean, where evidence was concerned, according to the news reports. Police were appealing for witnesses. Eighteen months had passed since he was found in a pool of blood in his office, and yet no one had heard a thing. It sounded like a professional job. Had Laura paid someone to take him out? If so though, would a hitman use a biro as a murder weapon? Wouldn't they use a gun? Maybe not, it was a busy area of town so someone would hear. A pen is still a very odd weapon though. Bex was getting ahead of herself now and she chastised herself out loud. Sarah had not returned her messages and she didn't know whether to give it one last shot to find things out about Laura or not. The Great Aunt gave her plenty to think about, but Bex couldn't ignore the fact that sometimes Ivy repeated herself and seemed a little senile so, how much of what she said could be relied upon?

Laura hadn't wanted to fall out with Sarah again. Sarah had threatened to throw Andrea down the stairs when she broke the news of her pregnancy. Carla felt sick to her stomach when she heard about this. It brought back memories of Alex trying to do the same thing to her. Carla reached out to Andrea and decided that whether Sarah came around or not; she couldn't leave the poor kid to deal with all this on her own. Her maternal instinct wouldn't let her leave this and she had completely agreed when Laura had ranted. Between the pair of them they could help iron this mess out surely? Sarah probably didn't mean it; it was clearly shock talking.

Laura had decided that she would also support Andrea. Sarah was dead to her now, how can mothers' treat their daughters like this? Laura didn't understand at all, but her heart ached for Andrea who was a scared kid with no clue how to look after herself, never mind a baby. Laura's own mother had been convinced her daughter would amount to nothing, but a pram faced teenager. How wrong she was. Laura was proud of her career, it might not be much to most, but Laura had worked hard to get where she had. Academically she had never been very bright, but she had to admit she had done alright for herself.

Carla put the kettle on, Laura had gone to collect Andrea who had got herself in a terrible state when they had spoken over the phone. Betty wasn't thrilled at the prospect of being a great grandma, but Andrea was her only granddaughter and Betty wouldn't let her down. She hadn't known about the pregnancy when she had left the house that morning; but Betty's mind had been put to rest when she had spoken with Laura who had agreed to collect Andrea and take her to Carla's for a bit while Betty was on a shopping trip. Andrea would be dropped off at Betty's when she was back home later. Until then Betty knew that Andrea was in safe hands, Laura may be unpredictable at times, but her heart was pure, and her intensions were good. She only wished she could say this of her daughter, what was Sarah thinking, scaring Andrea like that? As the head of the family, Betty would sort this out. Sarah was a good mother, she had reacted badly, but she must have been shocked. Betty knew that Sarah would never carry through with her threat.

Carla was nervous now; she had only met Andrea briefly at Laura and Glens wedding. The girl barely knew her and yet she had agreed to come and sit with the two of them. Carla settled Ella in front of the television, Cody, tired from the riding lesson and fresh air was now fast asleep on the sofa. Carla got a blanket for each of the children, and she tucked them both in snuggly, before returning to the kitchen. Andrea walked through the door and looked sheepishly at Carla. She had no idea what to say to Andrea, in the end though she did what came natural to her. Andrea hadn't pulled away from Carla's embrace and it was clear that while a hug couldn't solve her predicament, with a show of support, she could ease Andrea's mind for a short time at least.

Laura stayed silent as she sat at Carla's dining table. That table had been in Carla's old house and Laura had lost count of the amount of times that the two of them had spent sat here, putting the world to rights. No amount of talking would help Andrea though. Laura had been shocked to learn of her pregnancy, she was fourteen for goodness' sake! She should have been at home playing with barbie dolls or whatever the hell a fourteen-year-old should be doing. Laura wouldn't lecture. Mothering wasn't her forte, she had Carla for that. Carla would ask the awkward questions, Laura would just be here as moral support, but she hoped that Andrea would abort the child, after all, she couldn't work or go to college if she kept the baby. Laura felt that it would mean her taxes were going towards yet another lazy person who used their situation as an excuse to sit on their backside. Carla often remarked on how she wished she could work for a living. Laura thought this was guilt talking and that Carla simply wanted Laura to tell her it wasn't her fault and that she at least **did** work while she could. How Laura replied often depended on her mood and whether the biggest gay in the village had pissed her off that day. Laura felt that Carla sometimes did this to rub her nose in it, just as she did by mentioning the money which she had spent on designer shoes. Sure, some of them would be charity shop finds but not all of them were.

Andrea had made it clear that she wanted to keep the baby. Sarah had tried to talk her into pretending that **she** herself was pregnant; but Andrea didn't want to watch her mother struggle being a single parent to her own grandbaby. No, this was Andrea's burden and hers alone. Carla had said she wouldn't be alone in this. Andrea had learnt not to rely on anyone, her dickhead father had proved to her that all men are liars. Would Ben stand by her? She hoped so but Andrea was totally aware that men had the luxury of walking away. Whether Ben stepped up was entirely up to him, but this wasn't his first baby. He claimed the child's mother had moved away and he didn't know where they were. Andrea checked this out and within a matter of minutes she knew which area Ben's ex-girlfriend lived in, she was still living in Holt. The queasiness had returned now, and Andrea wasn't sure if it was her nerves at the thought of facing her grandmother; or if it was morning sickness. Whichever it was, she hoped it would do one.

Carla was drained from dealing with Andrea and as she had a quiet soak in the bath, she knew within a week these long soaks would be a thing of the past. Her new wet room had been designed now and was to be installed and ready to use by the end of next week. It would mean her bungalow would be like a building site for a few days, but she thanked the lord for the fact that the toilet was separate and would be sorted out first. Carla reminded herself that it would be worth it, and decided it was probably best that she didn't wind herself up. Ella wouldn't need to help her once she had the wet room. Her Saturday was interrupted as Bex waltzed in the unlocked door. "I'm in the bath but I will be along in a minute. The children's sleepy faces had appeared round the doorway and Carla promised they could have Chinese food if they ate it sensibly and then went to bed and straight to sleep afterwards. Cody's little face lit up. He loved food with a passion and the idea of having a take-out was such a treat for them. Carla often forgot that the children didn't get a Chinese, nearly as often as she did and, she vowed that from today, she would treat the children just as much as she did herself and Bex, although most of the time Bex paid and would actually be offended if Carla argued. The children were in their beds now, so the adult conversation could begin.

"All I am saying is that the old dear reckons that your lovely friend Laura isn't all she seems, I aren't saying she finished off the good doctor though. That may be a coincidence. All I am asking is that you be careful where she is concerned, at least until more is known about her. So far here is what I know to be true. I can't get a hold of

Amanda and Laura's parents seem to have vanished from the face of the earth too. Laura had allegedly been a patient of Doctor Steel when he was murdered. This is according to the great aunt, of course. Laura had been waiting to be discharged which, she wasn't thrilled about. She hadn't felt ready to be and she didn't want a different therapist. So far, Laura's nieces and their mother were missing. Okay, missing might be a stretch, Amanda wasn't answering the messages that Bex had sent, and Ivy hadn't heard from any of them since the day that Laura had turned up on her doorstep. She had announced that she had divorced her family because they were all liars. Ivy had done her best to calm Laura down and according to her she had only had telephone contact with Laura since that day. Ivy had called Amanda that day, there had been no answer. She had also tried to contact Laura's mother, to try and find out what had happened, again though, there was no answer and, texts had been delivered but not read." Bex took a sip of her drink now, Carla's face showed concern. It was clear to Bex now that Carla was beginning to wonder what Laura had said or done to them.

Carla was concerned for Amanda's safety now, the twins where abouts was unknown as well, it would seem; so, it may be wise to call the police and ask for a welfare check. She didn't know where they lived exactly, she only knew of the street name. She knew that Amanda had lived on the same street that their parents lived on. Laura had said as much one day when she was talking about their childhood. It was a mystery to Laura as to why Amanda wanted to be within spitting distance of those bastards. Why did she spend so much time there with her children? Who would want to expose them to that sort of environment? Amanda shouldn't have had children as she clearly didn't want to protect them, in Laura's mind.

Carla could remember this conversation vividly, she had thought that for a woman who didn't have children, nor want them, Laura sure was critical of how other people treat theirs. Carla had recalled collecting Laura for a night out many years before, when she had lived at home. They might have moved of course but Carla gave the address anyway. Would the police say she was wasting their time?

Laura barely mentioned them now, so Carla was forced to try and remember any piece of information that may be of use to the police. Was this a waste of time? Would they contact Laura? Carla had asked that they keep her name out of it. Having heard Bex out, Carla didn't feel that she could sit back and do nothing any longer, just in case something had happened to them. They might be in some sort of trouble. Or maybe they didn't want Laura to know anything about their lives, the Facebook messages Carla had sent had mentioned Laura in them after all. She blamed Facebook for her worry in a way. if Amanda was active on there then Carla would at least know she was alive and well. If Amanda didn't have a Facebook account, then Carla would have accepted that this woman valued her privacy but for them to remain unread and unanswered heightened her anxiety. Carla didn't think that Laura had anything to do with whatever this was, Laura didn't even speak with her family, so if they were missing in action then Laura wouldn't be aware of this. Furthermore, Laura probably couldn't help the police find out anything about Amanda, they hadn't been in touch for a long time now, Laura had tried to reach out to her sister, she had told Carla as much, but she hadn't mentioned to Carla if Amanda had replied or not. It was unlikely though, as both Carla, and Bex had tried, in vain, to reach Amanda.

Laura was shopping online, within a month Christmas would be here, it was to be her first one as a married woman. She knew that for now she must make an effort with the fat goofy kid. Glen wasn't bad looking, so her stepdaughter must get all the bad genes from her mother. This wasn't really about her; Laura was only making the effort because she knew it would make her look the bad bastard if she didn't at least try to make Glen happy. Her heart was saddened now as she realised that for the first year ever, she wouldn't be able to spoil her twin nieces. Amanda had a lot to answer for! Laura didn't know what to do, she could hire a private detective to try and track Calum, Tori and Tamzin down, It would open a can of worms if she did, and she didn't want to end up being caught for what she had done. Her brother-in-law may have them now but what if he didn't? What if they were in a children's' home? Amanda was a total failure in Laura's mind. Glen hadn't hidden the fact that he was thinking about wanting another child. Laura had told him that she didn't think it wise and that unlike other women, babies made her want to vomit. Unsure whether to give Glen what he wanted; Laura had agreed to consider it. Time wasn't on her side as she was so close to the menopause; she could practically feel her ovaries shrivelling up; so, she knew she better not take too long. The plus side to it would be that just like the fat goofy kid's drug addled mother, Glen would have to support any child that Laura had for the next eighteen years. If Laura got pregnant then Glen would have to put her ahead of the fat, goofy kid. This might be a worthwhile venture after all!

Carla was racked with guilt now; but she decided not to make Laura aware that she had asked for a welfare check to be done on Mr and Mrs White, as well as Amanda and her family. Her tummy was in knots as she waited, with her phone in her hand to hear back from the friendly police officer who had taken her call. She wouldn't be given specifics and Carla knew that, but they had said they would let her know when the family had been located, to put her mind at rest. Carla hadn't mentioned what Bex had said about Alistair Steel's death. She knew Laura, yes, she had a temper and Carla had seen her cry in anger many times, but this didn't make her capable of kidnap or murder or whatever else Bex suspected her of. Maybe a small part of Bex was jealous. With her busy work life, Bex didn't get to see Carla as much as Laura did and, before Laura had come back on the scene, Bex had been her only best friend. Then again though Bex wasn't the jealous type and she had never slated any of Carla's other friends. Carla didn't want to set Laura up, she was protecting her by not mentioning how Laura spoke of her therapist. She never mentioned his name though, she only referred to him as "the sexy doctor." Carla didn't want to make what would probably be a false allegation against Laura. If they hadn't got her as a suspect in Doctor Steel's murder, then it was because there wasn't any evidence to lead them to Laura.   Amanda would be tracked down and would have the twin girls with her, no doubt, Laura's parents would be contacted then Carla could tell Bex that she was wrong and that she needed to back off and leave this whole obsession with Laura, well alone. Though Carla loved Bex even she had to admit that when Bex had her mind set about someone, only proof of the facts, could change it. Carla couldn't admit to herself that she had an uneasy feeling about Laura, and this situation.

Bex felt satisfied now that Carla had called the police. There was tension here now, Bex had felt it when they had spoken about Laura. Bex didn't want to be right, being right that Laura had either frightened her own family into hiding or worse; might in turn, mean that Carla, Ella and Cody were in danger. Was it simply that Bex hadn't liked Laura? She had known that the suicide attempt was a ruse for attention, it had been a way for Laura to reconnect with Carla. The relationship that the two of them had, was intense to say the least. Bex hadn't liked Laura from then on. Having seen Carla through an actual mental health crisis, Bex couldn't help but wonder if faking one *was* a mental health issue in itself. After all, no sane person could lie about something so serious. From the off she had felt there was something sinister about Laura, and Bex would find out what it was.

Laura had snapped where Carla was concerned, she wanted to walk away from her, but she couldn't face being alone; sure, she was married but Glen didn't understand her the way that Carla did, but she had pissed Laura off again. She had only gone and spent £150 on each of the children for Christmas. Those ugly, spoilt little cunts didn't deserve so much as a selection box each! Laura had liked Ella somewhat originally, but as she was growing, she was more like Carla every day, both in her looks, and in her personality. Laura often referred to Ella as ugly, but she wasn't, she was beautiful. Laura was jealous of Ella and Carla's good looks. Laura had been at the award ceremony when Ella had been hailed a child hero. It was filmed for television and everything. Sure, Ella helped her mum dress and such things on her bad days but to call her a hero was fucking pushing it. Peter Andre had been presenting the awards, and Carla was wittering about looking fat! Laura told her she looked fine, though the devil on her shoulder had wanted to say something to the effect of: "Yeah that's because you **are** fat, not that he will be looking at you, have you **seen** his wife!" It was getting harder to resist saying things to hurt Carla. Laura knew their friendship was dying, just as she had known the same of her friendship with Sarah years before. She knew this was a pattern that kept happening, but it was beyond her control. It wasn't Laura's fault that her friends ended up doing shady things that Laura couldn't continually ignore. Part of her wanted to see Carla suffer and she wanted to witness this first hand. Eventually she would probably be as irrelevant to Laura as her actual family were. She picked up the phone, this would be the start of some beautiful karma which Carla more than deserved. Laura decided that if she suffered enough, then Carla may be able to stay in her life and avoid her sharing the fate of the *others.* The last time she had dished out some karma, by calling the NSPCC, she had also made herself look the hero. Bex had tried to steal her thunder, by helping Carla, but she hadn't physically been there, the way that Laura had. Those children were neglected. They were too young to be making their own lunches, while Carla stayed in bed, too lazy to even care!

It was Christmas week now, so the children were at home, which Carla loved. They had made bunting and baked cookies. The welcoming aroma of cinnamon spice hung in the air, and Carla's heart swelled with happiness as she reminded herself how lucky she was. The weather outside was miserable but beauty had a rug on which kept him warm from his ears down. Ella had still wanted to ride but Carla had persuaded her that it was a "do things indoors" kind of a day. They were halfway through rolling out the icing for the Christmas cake when Carla's phone rang. It was a work day but Laura was calling and as she answered Carla's heart was in her mouth, had the police let her know they were looking into the possible disappearance of Christopher, (Laura's father) Debra, (Laura's mother) Amanda, her husband Callum and their children Tori and Tamzin. Carla hadn't really had an update from the police only to say that Amanda and Callum didn't live on the street she had supplied and neither did Chris and Debra and that the enquiries were "ongoing". Now though, Carla wondered if they had let slip the fact that she had been the one to ring them?

"Hello?" Said Carla, her voice was unsteady, and she lowered herself gingerly into the large chair in her living room. It wasn't Laura, it was dialled from her phone, but it was a man's stern voice and for a second Carla panicked that Laura had been in an accident and that it was emergency services calling her. Then she realised she knew this voice, it was Glen.

"I am sorry to bother you but, well, have you heard from Laura?" Carla could tell that something was wrong by Glen's tone alone. She had only met him a handful of times but on those occasions, he had been jovial and spent the majority of the time laughing and joking. Carla hadn't ever heard Glen in a serious tone such as this, and she immediately felt her mouth go dry. Carla felt even worse now because Laura was missing in action. She and Glen had had a row about Christmas presents. Laura thought a £500 laptop was too big an expense for them, she had stormed out, but this had happened after Laura had drank a fair bit, she had taken her car keys and had drunk drove. Glen hadn't seen her since. Almost as an afterthought he had added, "Oh and she has a small hosepipe she took from the garage, not sure what she's going to need that for." Immediately Carla had felt her pulse race, Laura had always used pills as a means of trying to take her own life, but what if she had changed her weapon of choice, after all, pills had never came close to actually killing her before. She had always survived it, with no lasting damage. One thing that Carla knew though was that because it makes you sleepy, the method Laura was likely thinking about now, tended to yield results. "Have you called the police? They need to know that Laura has a history of mental health issues and that she is missing right now!"

Glen didn't think it would be worth calling the police. Laura was being a nasty, evil bitch and he didn't want to play into her hands by getting the police for them to try and find her. Laura wanted all the attention she could get, and Glen wondered now, would he have married her if he had found out what she was capable of before the wedding? He doubted so. He was sure, that eventually she would show up at Carla's, probably as though nothing had happened. Glen didn't know how much of this he could take! Laura seemed to hate her step-daughter with a passion. Glen had thought that it would pass, a lot of step-parents struggled to connect with their spouses' kids. He did love Laura, flaws and all, but he was sick and tired of her constant jibes against his only child. Though he knew Abigail wasn't perfect she wasn't a bad kid either and it seemed like Laura resented any gifts he bought for her. This hadn't been the relationship he had hoped for. They should all be close, like family. Blood didn't matter, did it? Laura had once mentioned that Amanda wasn't her father's biological child, but if anything, Chris loved Amanda more than he did her. Laura was complex, he hadn't realise this when he met her, she had seemed honest, with a "what you see is what you get" kind of vibe. Laura was like an onion and Glen felt he had only peeled back a couple of layers. This worried him because this stunt made him realise that he really didn't know all that much about her. He had never met a single blood relative of hers, although he had witnessed phone calls to Ivy, Laura's beloved Great Auntie. Why then was Ivy not invited to the wedding? Laura had said that she felt Ivy was too frail to be going out and would have to come in a wheelchair. That hadn't stopped Carla though. Glen didn't know what he could really tell the police about Laura. He was too ashamed to admit that he didn't actually know any specifics about his wife. Carla wouldn't let this lie though. Glen hadn't wanted the police to come, he would be forced to lie, this was because Glen had threatened Laura. He had taken a beating from her, but he couldn't not defend himself, he had marked her wrists and possibly her neck…

Carla couldn't understand why Glen didn't want the police to be called. She knew that, with the items Laura had taken with her, today could be the day that Carla lost her best friend. It was clear to Carla what she had to do. It was the second time this month that she had spoken with police regarding Laura. One minute she was practically accusing her of kidnap or worse and the next she was telling them Laura was her best friend who had complex mental health needs and had been missing a few hours according to her husband. Carla wasn't sure she could cope with this on her own, so she hastily wrote a text and sent it to Bex. She felt like she was in some sort of limbo where Laura was concerned. Why didn't Glen seem worried? He had sounded more like it was inconvenient that Laura had gone missing. Did Glen know something she didn't? Laura had just taken out life insurance. They had decided to try for a baby. Laura could be pregnant right now and Glen didn't seem to give a toss. The lines for the non-emergency police hotline had been jammed, so Carla dialled 999 and hoped that they would take her seriously. Laura was somewhere out there; she could be laid dying and she deserved for someone to care enough to want her found.

It was now Christmas eve and the hole that Laura's disappearance had left was massive. Carla knew she had to go ahead with Christmas for the sake of her children. They were with Carla's parents today; her parents hadn't really been there for her, their busy work schedules didn't allow them to be; but they had always been doting grandparents and for this Carla was truly thankful. She had spent the majority of the day wrapping presents, with her mobile phone sat next to her. She willed it to ring. This was always going to be a Christmas without Laura, but she was meant to be with her new family, learning for the first time the true meaning of Christmas, it is a time for families, whatever size or shape they may be. Her eyes filled with fresh tears. Carla was really struggling to keep it together, now that her children were out of sight the tears were uncontrollable. She hadn't been able to call or text Laura because Laura hadn't taken her mobile with her, Glen had said. The police had checked her card activity and she hadn't used it. This sent alarm bells ringing in Carla's head. The police had taken this seriously, in fact they had searched Glen and Laura's home. They had even searched the now vacant flat which had been Laura's. Carla's heart was heavy, and her mind was a world away from the wrapping. This usually was the time where Carla would be excited about what her children would think to the presents Santa had left under the Christmas tree, Carla had purchased a real one the previous week and had then worried because the pine needles were coming off a little quicker than she expected. Now though, all Carla wanted for Christmas was to have Laura back. She sat there truly heartbroken, there was no way that Laura would go anywhere without her bank card let alone her mobile phone, that thing was always glued to her right hand! She hadn't been on social media at all either, and again, this was something that Laura was never off of. She posted when she was happy and she posted when she was sad, in a lot of ways for a guarded person; Laura over shared her feelings on Facebook. Now though there was radio silence, which Carla found to be the biggest worry of all. She knew Bex had spoken with Laura's Great Aunt, could she be there? After all, when things had erupted with her family, Laura had turned up on Ivy's doorstep. She didn't know if the police had checked there, but, deciding she couldn't hang around for them to find Laura; Carla sent a text to Bex. She hoped that she might catch Bex on a break because the waiting around was killing her.

Bex had known by the way Carla's text was written that she was frantic, Laura had better have a good excuse for worrying her so. She didn't need this on Christmas eve! Did Laura even consider the children at all? They would know something was wrong, even if they couldn't pinpoint what it was. Bex had sent Carla Ivy's telephone number and she hoped that Laura was there, so that this drama ended before Christmas began tomorrow. Bex felt bad for feeling angry and she reminded herself that Laura could be dead and if that was the case, she would feel truly treacherous for hating Laura so much right now. Bex wasn't unfeeling, in fact she was quite the opposite, but she had never felt that Laura was genuine from that first time that she had sped down country lanes to get to her. Bex loved Carla too much to stand by and watch her be destroyed.

Carla had two worries now, one was that she had heard from the probation service that Alex was to be released in a week's time on licence and the other worry was that she had spoken with the police, who could offer no information relating to Laura. Carla had however, spoken to old Aunt Ivy, Laura wasn't there, and she had not heard from her in a few weeks. Ivy said that she felt guilty talking about Laura without her knowledge but that she could tell that Carla was beside herself with worry. That wasn't a lie, Carla hadn't slept at all in days, and she had exhausted every avenue when it came to Laura's Facebook friends. Sure, many of them had shared Laura's picture with heartfelt pleas for her to either return home or if she felt that she couldn't to at least make contact with Carla or the police. Ivy had passed on Chris and Debra's address and also Amanda and Callum's. Carla knew that she must leave the wrapping until the children were in bed later and she called a cab to Chris and Debra's. She knew that they would not have even heard of her from Laura, who admitted that she never shared details of her life with Chris and Debs. She hadn't a clue what to say to them, she had to see if they had any idea of Laura's whereabouts.

It didn't feel like Christmas to Glen, He had originally been angry at Laura, it was true that she had said some unforgivable things about his precious child. Now though, Glen reminded himself that though they had agreed to try for a baby, Laura wasn't a mother, and she was clearly finding the role of step-mother difficult. Glen had known he would be a suspect; the husband always is in cases such as this. Glen worried that Laura may have taken her own life. Her car had been found, by the bridge, which was a popular suicide spot. What if Laura had stopped to help another motorist and then they had kidnapped her? It did seem far-fetched, but the fact was that Laura had only lose change on her and she hadn't accessed her bank account. Carla had been her only real friend and she hadn't heard from her. If it wasn't for the fact that Carla had involved the police, then Glen may suspect that she was there.

Carla knew that if the police knew she was here they wouldn't be happy because this was an ongoing investigation. Laura probably hadn't contacted her parents, that wasn't why she had come, Carla didn't really know that much about Laura, they may have an idea of where to look. Okay, so they weren't the nicest of parents but still they may have something worth hearing. Carla knocked on the door of the large bungalow and there was no reply. A car stood in the drive-way. It was a BMW, a posh one at that. Unsure if they even used the front door, Carla followed the path round the back. She stopped dead in her tracks.... there was a trail of what looked like dried blood that led to a mound of dirt. It could be the blood of a cat or dog that a fox had dragged through, but the mound of dirt made Carla nervous. Should she call the police, or would they think she was being dramatic?

Christmas had passed in a complete blur for Carla, she couldn't stop seeing the blood in Chris and Debra's kitchen, she shouldn't have gone in there, but she wanted answers and she was sure that they were in there ignoring her, knocking at the door. The smell in the house was foul, it made her gag, it was like decay and rot. She had decided to get out of there and call the police. The sheer amount of blood alone had told Carla that whoever it had belonged to wasn't alive. She hadn't seen any bodies though. The police had come to her aid pretty fast, and they had driven her home. Carla was visibly shaken. She had kept checking the news all night, but nothing was mentioned about what she had found. Why were the police keeping this case out of the media? What if whoever had hurt

Debra and Chris had also hurt Amanda, Callum and their children? What if the killer had come back for Laura? Was money the motive? If Amanda and Laura were out of the picture who would inherit their parents' estate? Carla had no answers to these questions of course, she was worried more than ever for Laura's safety now. Why had Laura left with a hose pipe though? Had Glen been seeing things?

It was four o clock, three days after Christmas, when Carla's doorbell sounded. Daisy barked and wagged her tail, Carla felt so drained but suddenly her heart was hammering in her chest, she hoped beyond hope that this was Laura or at least some news about her....

The lady stood in the hallway, waiting for Carla to show her through to the living room. Sure, she had answered the door holding the handle on the spaniel's harness, but Fiona had worked for the Department of Work and Pensions for long enough to know that people are good at lying. Particularly those who want to screw as much money out of the system as they can. The complaint had stated that Carla had been seen competitively show jumping. Fiona hadn't seen any actual proof that she had, just a photo where Carla had been wearing a blazer, with what looked to be her daughter also in a blazer. The show had been rained off the day this person had claimed she had seen Carla riding. Fiona zeroed in on a picture of Carla riding a grey horse and her excitement was palpable. "This is you, is it not, on this photograph?"

Carla's eyes rested upon the photo on the wall, she remembered that day in detail, there were many times out on that cross-country course where her steed, Lulu should have refused or even fallen. Carla had been hungover; she hadn't even walked the course the night before! She smiled now as the memory came back to her. It was the year she had met Alex; he thought her horse riding skills were far better than they were. Her eyes came to rest on the gold writing where Her horse's show name "Friday Feeling" was written and below that, was the date. 12th September 2004. She knew now that she could prove that it wasn't a recent photograph. She was twice the size now for a start. She did ride but the truth was that Carla hadn't jumped since she fell pregnant for Ella, years before. Sometimes she only plodded around, it was almost like a form of physiotherapy. But Carla wished that she could work, that she could still compete.

Fiona felt stupid now, her excitement had made her overlook the fact that Carla wasn't a skinny woman nowadays and besides that, the photograph was dated. Carla had also made her aware that to compete on a pony, (which was all that beauty was) you had to be fifteen years old or younger. Fiona should have fact checked before she came here. She didn't know the first thing about horses and, had she known that to even sit in the ring you must be wearing correct show gear, she wouldn't have come here. Carla had clear disabilities; Fiona now wondered if someone was doing this to spite Carla, it hadn't been the only call they had received about her claim being false, but it had been the only call that mentioned specifics. Carla had told her she was more than welcome to call the place where Ella's pony was kept, to confirm that she didn't jump so much as a raised trotting pole. Fiona was annoyed now that a hoax caller had wasted her time.

Carla had resisted the urge to tell this Fiona woman that it wasn't a good time, because her big sister was missing, maybe even presumed dead at this point. The children had been good as gold and they were busy playing with their toys. Carla had been ringing around the hospitals in the area and not only giving Laura's name but also asking if there were any Jane Doe's who had either passed away or lost their memories or fitted her description. Laura wouldn't put her through this, Carla knew that she wouldn't. Every day the answer was the same, "No sorry, please try again tomorrow!" It was frustrating. Carla expected the same mundane reply today, but she was in for a surprise; "We've had a transfer of a lady who came to us last night from the big city hospital. She's had some sort of major head trauma some time ago and she has lost her memory; she had been at the big city hospital since the 24th, the poor love, had a brain bleed!" Carla explained that her best friend was missing and that she was sure something had happened, she wasn't next of kin, Glen was, but Carla was sure that Glen was as worried as she was now, so he might agree to check this woman out. She was around the same height and build, she had blonde hair, but then Laura never stuck to a certain hair colour, so that didn't seem to rule her out completely. She would ring Glen right away!

He had seen Carla's number come up, but in truth if Laura was dead then what good was it hoping for a better outcome. He did love her, but what if she had just left him, taken the hose to scare him so that he wouldn't dare tell the police and she had gone off to start a new life. The only thing that didn't make sense to him was why keep Carla in the dark? Glen knew that Carla was as loyal as they come and that if she knew anything about Laura, she wouldn't likely tell him. What was very telling though was the fact that Carla had told the police. For some reason from Christmas day onwards Laura's photograph was all over the local and even the national news. It seemed that the case was being amped up. Was it because Laura had missed spending Christmas with her little family or even with Carla and the children? Laura would never have spent the day alone. Carla seemed sure that the lady in the local hospital was Laura, it **has** to be her, she had said. Glen didn't want to be roped into this, but he was Laura's next of kin and he had married her for better or for worse! He picked up his van keys and set off towards Carla's house. They would drop the children off at the veterinary practice to spend the day with Bex on route. After all this could take a while to straighten out and if it was Laura would she remember him?

Bex didn't mind watching the children, they knew her staff and would be no bother playing in the back room with a puppy that had already found itself a casualty of people who had thought "a dog was just for Christmas not for life!" It saddened her but the puppy was healthy and had now been vaccinated, so Bex knew that she could find a home for the poor little thing! She knew Ella and Cody would love playing with the cute little bitch and they would be doing her a favour, The puppy had spent the morning crying for attention, and the staff were trying to play with her on their breaks. Bex hoped this was Laura, she had seen Carla briefly on Christmas morning and she looked an absolute wreck. The sooner the police got to the bottom of this the better. Laura was all over the news, morning, noon and night and had been for the past three days. Bex had begun to accept that something must have happened to her, or else Laura would have called the police hotline at the very least.

The ward was busy, and the nurse was clear that Glen and Carla could creep into the room to see if the woman in the side room was

Laura, if it was then they would both be allowed to stay, in the hope that she would wake up and remember them. If it wasn't then they were to leave and not mention the poor woman to anyone. The police may be coming in later to see this lady because hospital staff thought that she had been attacked as there had been blunt force trauma. Glen was going to go in alone because he would know if that was his wife in there but suddenly his legs felt like jelly. He wanted it to be Laura, if it wasn't then he and Carla would be no closer to finding her. Glen instinctively slipped his hand in Carla's which caught her unawares and she jumped slightly. Glen had forgotten until a second ago that Carla had post-traumatic stress disorder, caused by what her bastard of an ex-husband did to her, and Glen could have kicked himself.

Carla felt odd holding Glen's hand, she hadn't held a man's hand in a very long time; but Glen was visibly nervous. She was too, but if this was Laura then at least she was alive which was better than what Carla had been picturing. She peered around the door and her jaw dropped. Carla *knew* this woman, but it wasn't Laura. She had seen the profile photo of this lady on Facebook. This was Amanda! Carla shook her head at Glen who had only made it part way round the door. He looked completely crushed, he had then listened on in disbelief as Carla had explained to him that the woman in that bed was actually his sister-in-law. They went to tell the nurse that they knew the name of the Jane Doe and they passed on Ivy's telephone number; but that neither could be of any assistance. Carla had been keeping Andrea and Sarah in the loop. Neither of them was speaking to Laura by the time she had disappeared, but this was something that Laura had kept Carla in the dark about. Sarah and Laura fell out over Andrea, she knew that but now Andrea and Betty wanted nothing to do with Laura, though no one wanted to explain why. Still Carla knew that deep down Sarah was worried about Laura. She had said as much when Carla had rang her the day Laura had disappeared. Sarah did not want anything bad to happen to Laura, but she told Carla that she couldn't have her in her life either. She had been hurt by Laura too many times now.

When she had arrived home Carla had been preoccupied. Amanda had been found ;but she couldn't help to locate her parents, her husband, their children or her sister, amnesia meant that even if she had been awake, she wouldn't have been much use. The mystery had only grown. As soon as she smelled it, Carla knew what that smell was. The letterbox was wet, and the carpet was completely sodden. Petrol. She was pushing the intrusive memory away now and gathering the children together, with Daisy, as they exited as fast as they could.

Carla went to her neighbour's house, he kept himself to himself, so she had only met the old guy a week or so before. But she didn't care right now, this was an emergency! With everything that had been going on Carla had lost track of the days, it wasn't until a second ago that she realised that Alex was a free man. Her blood ran cold. How had he tracked them down so fast? Had he known that they weren't there? Would he come back later to finish the job? Carla felt like the only number she had really dialled lately was the police, but she had to report this because Alex wouldn't hesitate to burn her alive. She had hoped the children would be safe from him but apparently not.

Brian was an elderly gentleman who closed his curtains as soon as the sun went down, he locked his doors in the winter too. He was silver haired and a well-built man, but he was softly spoken, and he wouldn't harm a fly. He had been a little dubious as to whether he should unlock the door to see who was there. He hovered behind the curtain now fiddling with a set of keys….

Carla was screaming now, desperate for the safety of his home. Alex couldn't get to her there. Here though she felt exposed, if he was still around, he could have grabbed her and slit her throat, just like he threatened to do with Ella. Alex wouldn't have spent the past few years, regretting his actions that day. No, Carla knew him, he would have spent them plotting his revenge! Fresh tears formed as Carla tried to explain to Brian what had happened. He had called the police on her behalf and had passed her a box of tissues. " "Ey up lass, dry your eyes, you and the young 'un's are safe now." His Yorkshire accent was thick, despite the fact that Brian had lived in Holt since his mid-twenties. He told Carla this as they had a cup of tea and waited for the police. Brian enjoyed Carla's company, even if it had come about in a bizarre way. Carla had been completely retraumatised, that much was probably evident to Brian. She felt so vulnerable and not for the first time, Carla had wished that she still lived next to Sylvia Wilson and Jo Bainbridge. She had known that she was safe there. Her neighbours had always listened out for things and checked in with her, she loved her new bungalow, but she missed her old friends. Waiting for the police seemed to take an age. Carla would ask them what she could use to get the petrol out of the carpet, they might not know but she couldn't leave it like this in case Alex came back once they were all sleeping.

Brian had only met Carla and the children briefly until tonight. She seemed genuine enough, but the poor lass was going through so much. He hadn't realised until this evening that the missing woman from Norwich was his new neighbour's best friend. He had listened intently to the details of the case and felt that having found a seemingly gruesome scene, Carla was still no closer to finding her best friend. To top it off her ex-husband was a free man, and it was likely him that had soaked the letter box and carpet in petrol. Brian wondered if he would ever get a peaceful life again because Carla seemed to have brought a lot of drama with her to the quiet estate that had been his home for over sixty years.

Carla had used her carpet cleaner on the hall carpet and hoped that that would be enough to rid the house of the smell of petrol. She wouldn't sleep tonight; she knew that much. She was hypervigilant too afraid to go to bed in case Alex came back, she wouldn't hear a thing from the back of the bungalow. So, Carla had settled in the living room. At just gone one in the morning, she heard a light tapping on the window. Carla was completely gripped with fear; if it was Alex then maybe he was testing to see if she was asleep. Her head was thumping now as Carla gripped Daisy's harness for all that she was worth and made her way, gingerly to the front door to see if she could see anything.

The rain was really coming down now and Carla sure was taking her sweet ass time to open the door! It almost angered her visitor; didn't that dizzy old cow know that it was thunder and lightning? It wasn't an ideal time but then it wasn't like this visit could be made in broad daylight, was it?

Carla knew from the silhouette in the doorway that this wasn't Alex. She relaxed a little and quietly whispered "Who is it?" though she was glad it wasn't Alex; Carla knew that none of her friends or family would call at such a late hour. Usually, Carla would have been in a deep sleep thanks to the Temazepam that her doctor had prescribed. She had been flicking through the channels when she first spied the reporter stood on Cherry Grove outside the house that Carla had visited earlier in the week. She could see a crime scene tent in the side of the garden now. The scene she had found had been chilling, but Carla hadn't expected it to end with a murder inquiry! The reporter said that it was unclear how *many* bodies had been found, but that they were appealing for witnesses. Carla knew that the police had been aware that this was the home of Chris and Debra White, but she hadn't seen any bodies when she had been there. She certainly wouldn't sleep now!

Laura was nervous as she faced Carla for the first time, she had thought about telling Carla the whole truth but there were some things that Carla would likely not forgive her for, no matter what the motivation was. The kettle boiled and Carla was pouring the coffee, Laura was soaked to the bone, so Carla hadn't asked her if she wanted a drink she had just gone ahead and made her one. She turned to look at Laura and burst into tears, she was relieved to see that Laura looked to be okay. She longed to hug her, but Laura probably wouldn't thank her for it. "We must call the police, Laura. They have been actively looking for you; they even drained the lake where your car was found. I thought you were dead!" Carla's voice cracked now as she could hold the emotion no more. For over a week and a half she had been in limbo and with each passing day, the hope that Laura would be found alive had been diminishing. Carla allowed all the emotion to drip down her cheeks. Laura took a few steps towards her and wrapped her in the most meaningful embrace the two friends had ever had.

"You called the police and had them look for me? Didn't Glen call them? I thought he would have done given that he had pushed me to leave in the first place! I don't know if I want to be married to him anymore Carla. I just lost it, I can't cope with *lady* Abigail and what a spoilt little bitch she is. Glen will never side with me over her, and I just can't win. I get on with older kids usually, just like I always did you, but not her. She's a vile, ugly cunt sis and I just don't think I can be dealing with her anymore. I know you will have questions about where I have been and all that, and I promise you that you will get all the answers that you need. I just can't believe you *actually* called the police. I know we must call them, so they know that I am safe, but do you mind if I explain a few things first?"

Carla wanted answers, in fact she needed them, but the guilt was eating her alive now as she wrestled with whether to tell Laura about her going to her parents' house, which now was a crime scene, and how, because of Laura's disappearance she had accidentally found Amanda. Carla didn't understand why but for the first time ever she was afraid to be honest with Laura. Would she be mad that she had stuck her nose in? Yes probably, she would likely be happy to hear about Amanda though. The truth was that if she turned on a television, she would know that **something** had happened at the home of her parents.

Laura didn't want Carla to be angry with her, the truth was that up until the past few minutes, she had become resentful of Carla to the point of wanting to see her suffer. That was why she did the things that she did, but now everything had changed. Laura regretted the phone calls she had made regarding Carla. She hadn't done anything too awful, though she was sure that some of the agencies hadn't yet been in contact with Carla to follow up the complaints. The first call had been followed up; she was genuinely worried for Carla's children. They **were** neglected. On the days when Carla couldn't prepare a meal, Ella made cereals and toast. How is that a decent meal? Then she had of course claimed that Carla had been out competing. She knew that that phone call was wrong, but Carla shouldn't be allowed horses at all, and neither should her bratty little crotch goblins. She had also called the RSPCA, while Daisy was looked after well, was it *really* fair to make a dog be your slave? She couldn't admit any of this to Carla. She had gone missing to make Glen suffer and inadvertently she had ruined Carla's Christmas. That hadn't been intentional, in fact Laura did feel a little guilty now that she realised the impact all of the above had had upon Carla. Carla looked thinner, paler, and she had aged immeasurably since Laura had last laid eyes on her. Laura hadn't known why she wanted to scare the living daylights out of Carla, she was sure she would be caught with the petrol can, it hadn't been dark when she had done it. Laura knew that if Alex was free then he would be blamed for this, (and if he wasn't out yet, Carla would think he had organised it from inside) it was too easy in a way. Alex deserved all he got; he would deny it of course; but then he often lied to save his own skin. This time he would be telling the truth, just like the boy who cried wolf. The police weren't coming after Laura, she was a domestic abuse survivor, their own records would back this up. Glen had played into her hands months ago. "She had fled in fear for her life" she would say, her tummy felt full, even though she had barely eaten a thing since she had found out. Her tummy was full alright, full of baby. She was coming up to the three-month mark. This was why she hadn't been able to forgive Sarah about what she had said to Andrea. Laura hadn't a clue if she was going to keep this baby. It depended on Glen; one more wrong move and she would pull the plug on her pregnancy.

"First of all, I am upset that Glen didn't call the police himself; second of all, I had two glasses of wine and he hit the roof all because I am up the duff right now, and I admit that I panicked and ran! I met someone else at work and he took me to a hotel, all was paid for on his card so that I couldn't be tracked. I really don't know what I was doing. This being pregnant malarky isn't as fun as it looks, and I have doubts as to what it is I want. Glen wants a son, I thought it my wifely duty to give him what he wants; partly for him and partly so that he will defend me when the fat goofy kid starts shit with me, which makes me sound like a bitch, but honestly Carla she's lucky she's his kid or I would have decked her by now. I want to give him the son he always wanted. He's so excited about it. I will feel like a failure if it's a daughter but honestly, he won't mind. I told him I am only putting myself through this once. I didn't sleep with the guy from work until I left so its Glen's baby. I want to be motherly like you are Carla, I can't see it happening but then I haven't had the baby yet. I am sorry for ruining your Christmas and worrying you, but I didn't think you would be worried. Didn't Glen tell you I was pregnant? I never said I was going to kill myself or whatever and the police didn't really need to be called but I am so touched that you, at least cared enough."

Carla was relieved to see Laura, she was shocked about the baby and part of her was angry and she wasn't sure whether to be angry at Glen for lying about the hose pipe or to be angry at Laura who had at the very least, dumped her car by a local suicide spot. Only to return weeks later looking absolutely fine. She had yet to inform Laura of the crime scene that was plastered all over the papers. Maybe Laura would be able to assist the police with their enquiries. Amanda was now fully conscious, Carla had taken that call from Ivy earlier yesterday evening. But, due to the head trauma, Amanda hadn't been able to remember anything, other than the fact she had children and she thought she was married due to the wedding ring on her finger, which she was of course, but she hadn't remembered Calum. It was in the hands of the police now who had likely handed it over to Scotland Yard or similar. Holt was a small town really and it was ill equipped to deal with missing people and possibly a murder, or murders. Carla knew to tread carefully, the last thing she wanted to do was to spook Laura. She held back a little because of this and chose her phrasing meticulously. There were so many twists and turns to this, that Carla lost track of things at times and she couldn't mention Bex involvement or her budding friendship with Great Aunt Ivy.

Laura wasn't shocked about the police possibly finding a body; indeed, she knew they would likely find several, but then Laura hadn't been as careful as she was capable of being, this attack was different, it was frenzied, and she had to get away from the scene quickly. She knew how to feign shock, in fact her freedom demanded it. This wouldn't lead back to her, she hadn't ever given any clues about her family, not even to Carla. Sure, she had kept in contact with old Ivy, but no one would know that and with the old dear's memory deteriorating these days, she couldn't be relied upon to know what the truth was. Some people deserved to die; she was doing the world a favour. Debs and Chris were not good people, she was ridding the world of their evilness, and with Amanda gone no one would mourn them. Laura may even inherit their home. If she did, she would sell it and use the money as a deposit on a home as nice as Carla's. At least now Laura knew the police would be questioning her about it, so she was ahead of the game in a way. The last moments of Amanda's life had been too hard for her to witness. Amanda wasn't an intended target. She had been in the wrong place at the wrong time. She hadn't given her the quickest end either. Amanda had caught her, shotgun in hand covered in blood. There was no talking her way out of it. If Calum had any sense, he would be somewhere hot rebuilding the lives of his children, whose mother had "abandoned" them. She had been clever about how she had covered her tracks. Forging Amanda's handwriting was almost too easy, the letter stated that Amanda had found someone else. Now though Laura knew that the house of cards was falling and before long Carla would have worked out that the calls had been down to her, she knew she had to call time on this friendship, and it brought tears to her eyes.

Laura had been so shocked to hear that her estranged parents' home was an active crime scene, and while it was all over the news, it was currently, all speculation. Carla hadn't mentioned Amanda, Laura wouldn't be happy with her prying, she hadn't even told Laura that she had been to her parents' home. As she thought about this, the scenes of blood and gore came to her mind and she tried to shut them out as the memory of the smell of decay came into her thoughts, uninvited. Deep, deep-down Carla knew she didn't fully trust her "sister" now, if she did then Carla wouldn't have withheld information like she was doing. She didn't have to fear Laura; but then she was on her good side. Carla knew that to remain safe she had to make sure it stayed that way. Laura probably wasn't involved in this, and she could be the killers next target, so Carla chastised herself and resolved to keeping an open mind. It was late when she finally saw Laura to the door. They had called the police and told them how Laura had run away with a colleague to flee the violence that Glen might have dished out. Laura had wept as she told them that she worried for the baby she was carrying and that she didn't know whether she wanted to return home.

It had been several months since the murders had been on the news, and the police were keeping the details close to their chests. All that Carla had seen on the news was the fact that two bodies who were confirmed as Debra and Chris White had been found and that the crime scene had been a bloody one. Amanda's blood had been found there it said, but it was never put out to the public that Amanda had survived the ordeal. Carla had no idea whether Amanda was still alive, she knew that it was entirely possible that another bleed could happen to Amanda and her brain may not recover if that were to happen.

Bex had by now been very vocal about Carla watching her step with Laura. Laura had messaged Ella not so long back slagging off Carla, stating that "no one could be more ill than her fucking lazy, fat cow of a mother, didn't they even realise that she (Laura) had shut down to the point of not wanting to live?" Laura seemed to forget the person that she was texting was only a child, albeit a preteen with a mental age of about eighteen. Carla had forgiven her; stating that while pregnant Laura was off her meds, and this was another mental health crisis. Bex didn't for a second believe this but, since Laura had decided to end her marriage, Carla had felt sorry for her. Ella hadn't forgiven her though and she stayed in her room when Laura had visited from then on. Bex didn't know what Laura would do next. The police couldn't pin anything on her, by the looks of it. Neighbours hadn't heard a thing; they had been away on the days in question. The bodies were badly decayed which meant that an exact time of death couldn't be pinpointed. The White's neighbours had admitted when shown a photograph of Laura, that no one looking like that had ever visited Chris and Debra's home, to their knowledge. Bex knew in her own mind that Laura was guilty, but Carla was almost blindsided to the control that Laura had over her, it scared Bex that even after Alex had done what he had, Carla was still vulnerable enough for people to take advantage.

Laura was almost home and dry now. None of the murders could be pinned on her. She had wanted to be up close and personal when she took out her parents. She laughed to herself as she realised that most people who take their parents out do so to a restaurant not with a shotgun. Her father deserved the quick death she prescribed, with a bullet to the brain. She didn't offer Deb's the same fate. She instead shot her in the stomach and then dragged her out of the back door as she was dying, and she was still alive as Laura had filled in the hole. She had gone back for Chris and was filling in his grave as Amanda appeared. She hadn't had the chance to reload the gun, so she used the butt of it to cave her head in and she cried hard while doing so. One beautiful fact about tiny cul de sacs like Cherry Grove is that there aren't many houses, and you can see the whole street from one end to the other, this served

Laura well. No cars were in the driveways and Laura had knocked on a few doors beforehand, finding that the neighbours all seemed to be out. She had taken a clean set of clothes with her and made sure she was spotless before she left. She had wanted to check that Amanda was dead before she left but unlike with her parents, she didn't want the image in her mind of the light going out from Amanda's eyes. She had thought briefly about taking Calum, Tamzin and Tori out, but they were innocent. She loved Amanda but even Laura had to admit that Amanda was an enabler when it came to their parents. It was far kinder that her nieces just think that their mother had abandoned them for a new life with a mysterious stranger. Laura was almost cocky now. She had gotten away with murder, four times over. That made her a successful serial killer, a female one at that. This made her special. She wished she could brag about her accomplishments in one respect, but she wasn't going to get lifed off in some hell hole for that bunch of sadists. She would confess on her deathbed. She wasn't finished yet. If she did ever get caught of course, she would claim diminished responsibility and get carted off to Rampton. All the decent female serial killers went there anyway and hey, she would have curtains and a padded cell at least! The good doctor hadn't been any good at his job and he had said she had narcissistic personality disorder, Laura knew this couldn't be right. She wasn't cold, she did love people. She was just bad at choosing friends, she was likely too soft; and people knew it. If she *did* get caught then Doctor Steel's diagnosis would save her from prison, oh the irony!

Carla had forgiven Laura, but she hadn't forgotten how she had spoken to Ella on those texts. She wished she could. She still trusted her with her fears. Laura had been good to her of late, she had listened as Carla cried with worry about Alex coming and finishing her off. Carla could almost see how her life would end, with him, laughing like a mad man before he dropped the match that would extinguish her life. It filled Carla with a fear that she would have to see her children gasp for breath as the smoke took them away. Too young to have really had a shot at life. This terrified Carla so much that she had to be put on medication to calm her anxiety, but it wasn't enough to take it away all together.

Laura knew that she could get away with murder now. Alex was free, the homicides would be pinned on him. She would wait until she didn't need Carla, which would be soon enough. She was saving Carla from her pain, and ridding the world of two children, who over the years had infuriated Laura. Though they were older, they were still, spoilt, ugly, fucking cunts. It was 20 weeks that Laura had carried this child for, and with no intention of being a mother, Laura had only one option. She had known she would do this in the end. She had drawn it out with one cruel idea in mind. She wanted to be able to tell Glen the gender of the baby before she robbed him of ever meeting it. She knew that this would kill him inside, which was far easier than taking his life. This was legal too. Laura knew they would scan her before the procedure could be booked. She would tell them that she was unsure if this baby was what she wanted. She would act as though she was in two minds about it and ask the gender and for the scan photos. Only to call the next day to book the termination. Ripping the child from her womb didn't bother her in the slightest, but it would crush Glen who had been keeping in contact with Laura and asking about his unborn child. Since she had fallen pregnant, he had cared more about her than before and this attention had been nice; but Laura didn't want to work on her relationship with her husband, nor did she want to be a family. They had poured over naming books long after Laura had planned her revenge. She had seen the glee in Glen's eyes as he picked out boy's names, while she had picked out girls. If she could have destroyed her parents so legally, she would have done, but their deaths had been inevitable really.

Carla had just waved Laura off; they had chatted about Laura's latest landlady. Laura had moved in with Doris, as soon as she had returned to Holt. Laura had confessed to Carla that she believed this woman was abusing her only grandchild; inviting him in the bathroom as she bathed. Carla didn't know what to do because while it needed looking into it really wasn't her place. She had met the woman briefly a month or so after Laura had moved in there, and she hadn't got the feeling that something wasn't right. If anyone should report it, then it should be Laura. She tossed and turned in bed trying to make sense of the past few years she had spent with Laura. Laura wasn't vindictive, sure she could be spiteful, but only to those who deserved it. As a mother, Carla felt torn. Children should remain as innocent as possible for as long as possible; heaven knows the world is cruel enough. Her eyes were heavy, and she wanted to sleep, but just as she was drifting off her phone pinged. It wasn't a number that she knew, and the message made her blood run cold.

"I know where you are, which I know you have already figured out. Are the children in bed, I bet they are sound asleep? The end is coming, and you know it, but you won't know when. I will calmly sit back and watch as the flames burn the three of you to death, there will be no way out for any of you, believe me I will make sure of it, it's time to end your pathetic existence. You've led such a disgusting life, that even your own mother didn't want you. I had hoped you would just take all your pills and do me a favour, but selfish to the core, here you are, still fucking breathing, well not for long!"

Carla choked in shock; the tears were uncontrollable now. The worry she had about Laura's landlady was far from her thoughts; and she dialled 999 without delay. The police said they would try to find out if it was Alex, he had motive and he was certainly capable, but they had said they would try to trace the number. Carla didn't see much point in that. Alex was clever, it would be a burner phone. She finally fell asleep when the light was shining through the curtains. She knew Alex wouldn't be stupid enough to strike in the daytime. As soon as it was a more sociable hour, she would call Laura. Bex would be working, and she didn't want to worry her. Laura would be up soon to get ready for her "procedure" as she was calling it. Carla didn't want to worry her, but she had nowhere else to turn and Laura had been the one that had supported her through this. Carla felt wretched about calling Laura today and she would tell her she was thinking of her, if Laura was upset then Carla would leave it at that.

Laura had splashed out and bought herself new pyjamas and slippers for today. She had messaged Glen last night, firstly she had sent him the sonogram photos. Then she had told him she was legally murdering his son. She knew it would hit hard, Glen wasn't getting any younger and this was probably his last chance to have another child. It was unlikely that he would get with a woman young enough to give him a son now. It made her smile with the same glee that a sweetshop does to a child. Laura wasn't nervous or sad. She knew that she didn't want children, but she had needed a way of keeping Glen until she had sorted out other accommodation. This way she could do that, *and* destroy him, so it was a case of killing two birds with one stone. Ugh Carla had phoned. She knew what today was, but she couldn't let Laura have the sympathy could she? What better way to get people sending Laura messages of support was there? Ah, social media. A quick Facebook post should guarantee some instant sympathy. She wouldn't be cryptic like Carla was. Laura was never the sort to do that and have people writing "inbox me hun." Laura was far more direct. "Well folks, that's it I am going to go in for my procedure this morning. No more baby, I, unlike some, will not bring a child into a violent situation, so this is the start of my new life." Almost immediately the comments came rolling in. They were all supportive and most had wished her good luck today. She didn't have Glen on there, this wasn't about **him**, this was all about her. Okay, so he had only been violent on one occasion, most of the violence stemmed from her, but then she hadn't said who was violent, so, it's not like she was lying. Laura had thought about Abigail and whether to go after her next. It would look suspicious though, which is the only reason that Laura was allowing her to live. She would however be messaging her later and telling her exactly what she thought of her. Carla was safe, for now but Laura knew she was next. She just needed to bide her time first. Laura needed to set up a new best friend before she binned the last one. Sarah was done with; she wouldn't be backtracking with her. She had started to get close with her landlady, she often called her bitch tits when she spoke about her to Carla because she didn't want Carla to know that she was getting close to Doris. Carla had plenty of friends, Laura only had her. She wasn't done with Carla yet. It had infuriated her when the claims of benefit fraud hadn't stripped Carla of her income. She could have witnessed that and then she wouldn't have to actually kill her. She had the edge with this one. She knew who she had to frame and how to make it stick. She would get far more sympathy when poor old tragic Carla was killed, Laura would be able to get sympathy for a lifetime over it. Carla's whole life was tragic, its only right that her death would be too. Laura got dressed and then she called Carla.

The phone woke Carla from her sleep, she must have nodded off. The children were awake now, Carla could hear them, so she kept her tone as evenly as she could. The last thing she wanted to do was panic Ella, who at her age was only too aware of what her father was capable of, so Carla didn't want to alarm her. Were it not for the petrol a few months before, she would have thought he was bluffing. He still might be of course; but she knew better than to risk it. Carla had asked about Laura, who from what she could tell seemed completely fine. There was no nervousness to her voice, and she had listened intently to Carla as she explained about the text that she was sure came from Alex. Carla hadn't mentioned going to the police, she wanted to downplay the whole sorry event so that Laura wouldn't be worried about her and the children.

Laura said goodbye and pulled on her coat. She had finished getting ready while Carla was on speakerphone and was now nearing the hospital. She loved anaesthesia, it was better than any drug Carla had and though Laura wouldn't feel like she had had a rest it was something she always revelled in. Of course, if she hadn't waited it would only have taken a simple pill, but Laura preferred this, Glen would be hitting the booze today and it brought her great joy to picture it in her mind. His agony was the last thing she thought about as the medication took hold, when she woke, she wouldn't have the sickness that had blighted her life of late, she would be free.

Amanda hadn't slept, fragmented memories had begun to surface, she couldn't quite put it together and even if she could, would the police be interested in the mixed-up memory of a brain injured woman? She had attended a funeral which her aunt kept reminding her was that of both parents. Chris wasn't her real dad; Ivy had said, but he loved her even more than if she were his own. Her dreams showed her drag marks in red and she was sure it was a body, but she couldn't make out whose body; nor could she make out who or what was pulling it along. The therapist kept telling her to give it time; but Amanda grew frustrated and angry at herself, the police had told her that her parents were murdered, and that the murderer was likely the person who had attacked her, but they couldn't be sure. Amanda's darkest fear was that she had snapped and killed them, but then how had she herself been hurt, had they fought for their lives? What if time was something that she didn't have. She had noted the gold band on her finger, where was her husband and where were her children? Her medical records had confirmed that she had been pregnant twice, but some days Amanda didn't know if this was true. If she had, had two daughters why couldn't she remember their births? Why didn't she recall getting married? Were it not for her wedding ring would she doubt that too? She knew her name and she had grainy memories but nothing that was clear. If what the police and doctors said was true, then where were they? She was in hospital still and she would likely need care when she returned home. Where was home? Amanda hoped that being there might offer up some clues as to who she was as a person, she couldn't wait until tomorrow to be back there, and yet she was afraid of going home at the same time.

Laura woke up and looked down, there would be no scar, they would have removed the thing from the other way in. She was almost upset to not have a physical scar. She had collected many from horse riding accidents and motorcycle crashes back in the day. She wore t-shirts so that she could show them off, it often was a conversation starter, particularly as she didn't really know how to start one otherwise. She would be out of here in an hour. The doctors had told her not to drive herself here, but she had done, it wasn't far, and she didn't want to get into some scabby black cab to get back. her landlady, Doris, had offered to take her, but Laura had declined, she didn't take favours from anyone. She would stop off at Carla's on the way home. Laura wanted to see her in person, the way she had been on the phone was disappointing to say the least. She hadn't had terror in her voice when they had spoken over the phone and she must be afraid, hell Alex was a psychopath who always came good on his threats. Laura had guessed that the crotch goblins must have been awake when she had spoken with Carla earlier. One thing that Laura knew for sure about Carla was, that when someone is there with her in person, she's more likely to crack. She didn't feel gleeful about this though because Carla had given her plenty of sympathy this morning, it made Laura want to like her. She would soon have to call time on their friendship, regardless because this was what Laura always did, she moved on to the next victim after severing ties with the previous "sister". It had always been that way; she had warned Carla years prior that eventually someone gets too close, and she moves on. Sometimes to an old acquaintance and sometimes to a brand-new friend.

Carla made her and Laura a cup of tea and opened up the lounge. She and Laura usually sat at the kitchen table but today she knew her best friend needed the comfy leather sofa. She spied Laura secretly; trying to gage how she was doing without her knowledge. She really couldn't be fine after the operation she had just endured, surely? Laura did seem to be in good spirits, excellent spirits, actually. Carla went over the text again as she choked back tears. She wasn't just a little afraid, she was beside herself with terror and worry. Laura hugged her as she cried and sent the children off to play in their rooms. Carla was wracked with guilt, she had gone ahead and had children with a monster and though she had freed herself from his clutches; he was free now, free to text her, free to threaten her and free to kill them all.

Laura had listened while Carla went on and on about Alex, she made sure her face showed far more concern than she actually felt. Alex was lucky, he was free from Carla's moaning, which is more than could be said for her. She was through with biding her time now. She would have to move fast before her temper spilled over and she left a crime scene that was as frenzied as her family's demise. Laura hadn't attended the funerals, sure she wanted to; if only to witness the grief she had caused, but that wouldn't be smart. Laura was smart, she knew that the police would attend, she had seen so many murderers that were caught that way. She hadn't contacted her Aunt Ivy either, that would have made her look guilty. She knew better than to contact her after months of radio silence. The old bat certainly had a hole in her bag of marbles anyway. As soon as she had recovered physically from the operation, she would end Carla's little family's lives. First of all, she had to somehow bump into Alex, seemingly by accident. Nothing yells murder more than a violent ex leaving something at the scene of the crime.

Two days after she had called the police, Carla got another message, similar to the last. It was sinister; it read: "Two more days...." The police had told Carla to try and keep the offender answering but not to anger them. While she sat inside the sanctuary of the local police station, they had experts trying to trace which cell tower the text came from. It was unlikely to tell them much but then Carla had a brainwave. She sent a purposely scrambled message about her dropping the phone and being unable to read the text. Whoever this is can you reach me on messenger, that way I can read what you're saying. Ten minutes went by and then Alex's name showed on her messenger. The message read the same as the one that had been sent before. Now the police could trace the I.P. address and haul Alex in.

Carla was on high alert since returning home, as her mind took over and she was forced to withstand flashback after flashback of the abuse that she had suffered, thanks to Alex. She was trying to fight them off so she could remain present and as she came round, she realised her phone was ringing. It was an unknown number, which these days filled her with dread. She knew she had to answer and the relief she felt as the caller identified themselves could probably have been seen washing over her face. It was the police. "Are you sitting down Carla? We have traced the I.P. address to a place on Westside view. Carla felt bile rise in her throat. We have arrested a Laura Wade. She has admitted covering the letterbox in petrol and making threats against your life and the lives of your children. We are going to give her a caution and let her go with an order that she isn't to come to your address. I wouldn't contact her if I were you but that is up to you. She is remorseful and is saying she's had a lot on and isn't in her right mind. We have checked and found this to be the case which is why we have decided not to have her before a judge. She said you two were very close, she can't explain why she has done this. If you get anymore threats ring them in but I can't see it myself, good day!" Carla didn't know if she was in shock or what, but she felt like someone had stabbed her in the heart. Why would Laura do this? Grabbing her phone, she pinged a text to Laura.

"I just want to know why? Why would you be so cruel? I cried to you about these threats, I trusted you, I won't contact you again, I just need to know why?"

Within two minutes there was a whole paragraph back from Laura.

"You are a drain on society, it's always about you, isn't it? Oh, you can't work? Rub my nose in it why don't you, you spend my taxes on shoes and make up and pets you can't look after, why the

R.S.P.C.A. let you keep Daisy I will never know. Oh, and Social Services let you keep your children, who you basically treat like slaves. Is the penny dropping? I called them all. Your own mother can't love you, that says so much. Just do the world a favour and end your sorry existence, I will help if you can't bear to do it yourself. Better still walk out in front of traffic, oh that's right, isn't it? You can't walk, but you could breed, couldn't you? Leave me alone because if you don't, I will make good on my threats and I will watch you all burn, you twisted horrible bastard, How dare you have the audacity to ask me why! Fuck off and FUCKING DIE!"

Carla wished she was capable of being cold now but that wasn't her nature. As she sat there in shock she started to think about Doris. Laura had accused her of animal abuse and worse when she spoke to Carla. Should Carla warn her before it was too late? Much as she might want to, Carla didn't want to anger Laura further. Now she saw what had been right under her nose, Rebecca's words came back to haunt her. Maybe Laura was capable of hurting Amanda and worse still, killing people. Why had she not killed Carla, was it just threats? In a way Carla was scared of digging around in Laura's past and yet in another way if Laura was a killer, then she needed to be locked away. Carla's mind was racing, her mouth was dry, and her eyes were full of tears. She wasn't angry, she felt betrayed and heartbroken that someone she had known for decades could be capable of such cruelty. She cried out, like a wounded animal. She hadn't thought that friends could be the ones to break your heart, this way. Carla decided to sleep on it.

Bex was pleased that Laura had been found out, though it pained her to hear Carla cry like this, like a wounded animal screams out when caught in a hunter's trap, that is exactly what Laura was, a hunter who played with her prey. Bex wanted Carla to live with her, she had already got builders erecting suitable accommodation on her estate.

Laura went home to an empty house, Doris and the dogs were away for the weekend, they wouldn't be home for two days. Laura ordered a pizza and sat in her dressing gown. She couldn't finish Carla off now. The police would be on to her. Then again, they hadn't found Amanda's body and she had left her dying right beside her parents' rotting corpses. The police couldn't find their way out of a paper bag. Laura had not banked on Carla being clever enough to trick her into giving away her I.P. address though. It angered her, so much so, that without meaning to Laura had dug her fingernails into her palm. Still, a caution wasn't bad to say she had gotten away with four murders. Sure, Laura's record wasn't clean, but it wasn't a big deal. She would just have to stay in her present job with the most annoying gay in the village, for a bit longer until the caution had gone from her record. Laura had texted Doris and told her that Carla had goaded her and then played the victim. She had also said that Carla had been making out that Doris kicked her dogs. Laura knew that she had to say this so that if Carla ever mentioned that Laura had said it, then Doris would think she had turned it onto Laura to make her look bad. Of course, it was true, or at least Laura thought it was, she was losing touch with reality now, so it was hard to tell. They had a common enemy in Carla, a sacred bond to solidify their friendship. she could probably get Doris to do her bidding for her. Bitch tits did mistreat her dogs, but Laura wouldn't report it. The garden couldn't be seen from outside, she wasn't stupid enough to drop herself in it. It's not like Laura could really judge anyway, she was a murderer for god's sake. Laura knew that eventually she would turn on Doris, but not for a few years yet. If she played her cards right the old bat might be persuaded to leave her a chunk of money in her will. It wasn't Laura's fault that things ended this way, she had bad taste when it came to friends and lovers. She was just too soft, and people took advantage of her. All of her friends had used her as a taxi at some point and they all did shady things that she couldn't ignore. Laura had never been reported for her threats to any of them, until now though. She hadn't hidden her identity when it came to the others. Laura hadn't wanted to kill any of her previous friends, only Carla and her ugly fucking despicable sprogs. The night went on this way with Laura being peaceful and happy to her being angry and feeling vengeful. She yoyo'd until she fell asleep next to the pile of empty pizza boxes. She needed to keep her strength up to get her through the next few days.

Carla typed a carefully worded message to Doris which included screen shot after screen shot of Laura's messages about the old lady. Doris was shocked and heartbroken and while it brought Carla no joy to do it, she couldn't sit back while Laura did the same to her as she had to Carla and many others before her. Doris would have to wait until her daughter could be with her to confront Laura. She couldn't refute what Carla had said, there was proof. Doris knew that she would have to ask Laura to move out with immediate effect. If she did so while she was away, then Laura might damage her property.

Carla had written a cryptic post about Laura without any specifics, and the inboxes from many other previous "friends" of Laura's came flooding in. She wasn't shocked really; she knew now that Laura had hidden depths. Many began with," if this is who I think it's about she's done similar, to me", and tale upon tale of Laura destroying people's lives with false allegations of child neglect, benefit fraud and animal cruelty, to name but a few, followed.

Carla arrived at the city hospital with Bex in tow. Aunt Ivy had wanted to collect Amanda, but with her age, and with her own memory being bad, Bex couldn't very well leave her to it so, until Amanda's husband was traced, both she and Ivy would be staying at Becca's house. She knew it was nothing to do with her really, but over the last few years, Bex had grown fond of her weekly chats with Ivy. When Ivy had told her that Amanda was coming home but that Ivy had been told she couldn't care for her, Bex had felt it her duty. Now more than ever she thought Amanda's injuries were caused by Laura, though she knew not to mention it. Amanda's memory was fragile, at best, and Bex knew that there might be a chance that it never returned. She hoped it would. If it wasn't Laura then there was a serial killer on the loose and, if it *was* Laura, she might get away with it, but only time would tell. Bex had hired a private dick to try and locate Calum and the girls. She hoped that they had made it out alive. Appeals for them to call police had gone unanswered, but then they weren't forced to still be in England. Amanda could now wash and dress herself and she had the ability to remember things from after the incident. Bex was overdue some time off and had booked three months off work. She was going to do what she dreamed of, she bought an ex-racehorse, Called Chance. Carla moved beauty to Bex's house and packed up her old home. The new bungalow was ready, in the grounds of Becca's estate. Here, she could live freely, knowing that the road was private. The electric gates and CCTV ensured her safety.

Amanda was getting stronger every day, and she was truly thankful for Bex and Carla's help. Her memory was piecing things together and it could happen at the most random times. The most important one happened while Amanda was in the mirror fixing her hair. She saw her face and it reminded her of her sister. She hadn't realised that she had a sister at first but now she saw and fully recognised Laura, dragging the body. Amanda was upset but didn't want to scare the flashback away; so she sat on the bed and waited. Debra's body was in the ground, in the flashback she was frozen to the spot as the gun hit her and hit her, again and again, until it went black. "Bex call the police, I have remembered something!"

Laura *really* hated Carla now, she was homeless and aside from a married man she was sleeping with she had no one, and nowhere to go. As it happened, she needn't have worried about being homeless. Within minutes of her sitting in her car in the tiny cul de sac she was surrounded by police, her car was blocked in before she even knew what was happening. It was a shock as she sat in the police interrogation room. She had worn gloves when she murdered them all. Apart from the Doctor of course but then they didn't have her fingerprints on fi…. Laura's stomach fell out through her knickers, she was fingerprinted over mere threats to kill and that had been her undoing, when it came to Doctor Steel. Ah well, it's one murder and she could always claim diminished responsibility, after all, the good doctor himself had diagnosed her with a personality disorder. Soon she would learn that loving Amanda too much to watch her die had resulted in Amanda living. Something she would regret for the rest of her days.

Amanda had given her testimony and the court case was over, the sentencing was all wrapped up. The judge had several psychiatrists write reports and do assessments on Laura; and all had deemed her sane and culpable. Amanda held Calum's hand throughout. Her amnesia had stopped her from remembering him for months, all she knew was his name back then, but the private dick came good, and Calum flew back from Malta with both of his daughters. He nursed his beloved wife back to full health, with the help of Ivy, who now lived with them.

Carla knew she would never have to look over her shoulder, as in a shock move for the United Kingdom, the judge deemed that Laura Wade should spend the rest of her natural life behind bars. She currently resides at a prison as notorious as she is, in Derbyshire. Where fights are often ignored by guards. Carla wouldn't dwell on that, she and her children had lives to lead now, and they wouldn't waste a second. The children were never aware of how close they came to a killer, but Carla was, and it only made her grab life with both hands and embrace it, all the more.

Bex had put things together just before the police had, were she not so happy in her work, Bex might have thought about a change in career! Pleased she and Carla could keep one another company, they got to spend many nights laughing, until their sides ached. Daisy loved her long walks through the estate with Primrose, who Bex had found outside of her practice years before. The children had grown attached to Primrose that day, that she had looked after them at her work; and Bex never could say no to their pleading little faces. Even as they entered adulthood, Bex was still a soft touch on them, just as she was to Danielle.

Glen had found happiness, (despite Laura trying to destroy him.) with Sarah. As soon as his divorce from Laura came through, they married. Carla had been a bridesmaid. Andrea had given birth to a son, Jamie, who she and Ben raised together, with the help of Jamie's doting grandparents, Glen and Sarah.

Carla didn't trust anyone now, but then she didn't need to, Bex was all the friend she needed. She didn't feel a scrounger anymore either, because the book you have just read was a best seller, written by Carla herself.

Laura slammed the book shut. She couldn't believe that Glen had married Sarah or that, the people that she had brought together, were all successful, and playing happy families. What about Laura, where was the family that she deserved? She was fuming. Her cell was the only place that she felt safe. Even in here, big Tracey might get to her. It was no fun being a butch dike's little bitch.

Printed in Great Britain
by Amazon

85564679R00086